The
Wings of Ruksh

The Dragonfire series:

The Wings of Ruksh

Anne Forbes

Kelpies

Kelpies is an imprint of Floris Books

First published in Kelpies in 2007
Third printing 2016
© 2007 Anne Forbes

Anne Forbes has asserted her right under
the Copyright, Designs and Patents Act 1988
to be identified as the Author of this Work.

The publisher acknowledges subsidy from
Creative Scotland towards the publication
of this volume.

 This book is also
available as an eBook

British Library CIP Data available
ISBN 978-086315-602-1
Printed and bound by Gutenberg Press Limited, Malta

To my husband

Contents

1. The Loch Ness Monster

"Funny mist this," Duncan Campbell muttered, shipping his oars and trying to peer through the thick whiteness that lay heavily over the waters of the loch. "Eerie!" he added, shivering slightly. "A bit like old horror films. Thank goodness this is Loch Leven and not Loch Ness, eh!"

George Tatler smiled at his remark as he put his fishing rod to one side and reached resignedly for his flask and sandwiches. The day, bright enough to begin with, was now a complete disaster as far as the competition was concerned, for the mist, swirling down from the surrounding hills, had swiftly enveloped all the little craft bobbing in the loch.

The third man in the boat looked at Campbell in amusement. "You surely don't believe in the Loch Ness Monster, do you?"

The obvious note of disbelief in his voice riled the younger man into an unconsidered response. "I *do* believe in it, as it happens," Duncan countered somewhat irritably as he brought the oars in. "You see ... I've actually seen it!"

Tatler raised his eyebrows and studied his companions of the day with interest, for as it happened, the three men in the boat were all complete strangers. The tall, dark-haired man seated in the stern had introduced himself as Archie Thompson and although he'd said he was a policeman, Tatler knew he was Sir Archibald Thompson, Edinburgh's Chief Constable. Nothing wrong, he supposed, with a bit of tactful evasion. After all, hadn't he, an obscure but high-ranking

member of government, described himself as a Civil
Servant and met the Chief Constable's measured stare
blandly as he'd said it. The third man, Campbell, who'd
made the remark about the monster, seemed pleasant
enough. Young and fit, he'd admitted to being a photographer as well as a passionate angler and had immediately gained their approval by offering to row the boat.
So there they were; three men in a boat.

"You've seen the Loch Ness Monster?" Although
Tatler's voice was neutral, he raised his eyebrows
slightly as his eyes met those of the Chief Constable.
"Why don't you tell us about it?" he invited, waving his
sandwich vaguely. "We won't be doing much until this
mist lifts. We've all the time in the world."

Duncan Campbell pressed his lips together and
wished he hadn't opened his mouth, but the fact
remained that he *had* seen the Loch Ness monster.

He poured coffee from his flask and warmed his
hands on the cup before he began. "Look," he said
somewhat abruptly, "I don't expect you to believe me
and I've no real proof of what I say but last year, at
around this time, I was one of a team of photogra-
phers that manned the cameras round Loch Ness for a
Japanese expedition."

Tatler nodded. He vaguely remembered reading
about it.

"They were hoping to find proof of the monster's
existence, of course — and, like you, I thought it a bit
of a waste of time. But I was hard up, it was a job and
the conditions were fair. They employed several of us
and provided us with tents and the like. One morning, my turn for early duty came round ... the cameras
had to be checked regularly, you see ... and it was just
after dawn when I got up. As I left my tent, I automatically looked over the loch — and there she was! Nessie

herself, swimming towards the shore! Well, I knew the cameras would be recording everything so I jumped into my car and shot off along the road to where she would make landfall."

"And did you manage to see her close up?"

"Well, I would have done if it hadn't been for the sheep."

"Sheep?"

"The road by the side of Loch Ness tends to wind a bit but I had almost reached the part where it runs really close to the shore when I was held up by a flock of sheep. They were milling about everywhere and I couldn't move through them until the chap who was driving the transporter managed to get them all back on board again."

"Transporter?" the Chief Constable's eyes sharpened.

"Yes, you know, one of those huge things that are used to carry sheep. I don't know why it was there. Perhaps the rear doors were faulty or something, but the sheep had managed to get out and they were everywhere."

"So you didn't manage to see the monster again?"

"Oh yes, I did!" Duncan grinned suddenly. "I wasn't going to give up that easily! I opened the sunroof and climbed on top of the car to get a better view." He reddened and looked embarrassed. "Look," he said frankly, "you don't have to believe what I'm going to tell you and, quite honestly, I wouldn't believe it myself if I hadn't seen it with my own eyes. At the edge of the loch I saw the monster and not only that ... I saw a dragon as well."

"A dragon!" The boat rocked slightly as the Chief Constable sat up abruptly.

Tatler looked at him with renewed interest and on seeing the concentrated attention he was now giving to the photographer's words he, too, began to listen more carefully to what he had, quite frankly, been about to dismiss as a bit of a tall story.

"It *was* a dragon," Duncan affirmed. "A beautiful creature, red and gold, with wings. But the strangest thing of all was that there were people down there as well. I couldn't see them clearly from the car roof but I saw them later on when I watched the film. The cameras had picked them up, you see. At the time I thought I glimpsed a woman, but I must have been mistaken for the film only showed two men and two children. One of the men was the driver of the transporter."

"I'd be interested to see that film," the Chief Constable interrupted.

"It is interesting, actually. Not for what's on it, but for what isn't."

"What do you mean by that?" Tatler asked.

"Well, the film only shows the two men and the children at the side of the loch; the dragon and Nessie don't appear in it at all."

"But you saw them?"

"Oh yes! Nessie was a different type altogether; quite ugly and by far the bigger of the two."

"What happened next?"

Duncan shrugged. "Not a lot really. The dragon and the monster swam out into the loch and dived under the surface and the men and the children came back up to the transporter. Unfortunately, I stepped on the horn when I climbed back into my car and that alerted them. Until then, I don't think they knew I was there at all."

"You weren't, by any chance," interrupted the Chief Constable, "a passenger on the London Shuttle last year, were you?"

"The Shuttle? What are you talking about?" Campbell was genuinely mystified.

"Strange as it may seem, as he came in to land at Edinburgh Airport one night last year, the captain of the London flight reported seeing a dragon. Many of the passengers saw it too and I . . . wondered if you'd been among them."

"I didn't hear about that," Campbell said, frowning.

"There was a bit about it in *The Scotsman,*" the Chief Constable said seriously, "although they didn't actually mention a dragon. I think they called it an 'Unidentified Flying Object' or something of the sort. I suppose it *was* all a bit hushed up," he admitted a little ruefully, "although no great secret was made of it. Understandable, really! It wouldn't do British Airways any good to have their captains seeing dragons all over the place."

"But it *was* a dragon?"

"Oh yes! We know that because one of our special constables was on the flight. It gave him quite a turn. According to his report, it was straight out of the pages of King Arthur. Mind you, it could have been one of those mass hallucination things because nothing showed up on radar. They scrambled a jet to investigate but by then it had disappeared."

"Disappeared?"

"We think it landed on Arthur's Seat and we had the whole of Holyrood Park sealed off within minutes. Police patrols went over it with a fine toothcomb for days afterwards."

"Did they find anything?" asked Tatler.

As the Chief Constable shook his head, Campbell hazarded a guess. "Perhaps because the dragon had already gone to Loch Ness?"

"Well, if it did, it certainly didn't fly there! We not only had people scanning the sky but every vehicle that left the park was checked within ten minutes of the sighting. It so happens that the only one ..." and here the Chief Constable's tone altered and he paused and cleared his throat, "... the only one capable of carrying anything like the size of a dragon was ... a transporter full of sheep!"

The boat rocked alarmingly as Duncan Campbell leapt to his feet. "So *that's* where the dragon came from!" he said excitedly. "It must have been in the transporter!"

"I'm sorry to disappoint you, Campbell, but I was there when my men opened up the back of that transporter. There was no place in it for a dragon to hide and even if there had been — can you imagine it? The sheep would have been climbing the walls."

Duncan sat back in disappointment. "Look, I *did* see a dragon," he assured them seriously, "but I've honestly got nothing to prove it. If you see the film, you can only make out the men and the children."

"I'd very much like to see that film, Duncan. Do you still have it?"

Duncan nodded. "Yes, I have, actually. I made a copy of it for myself."

A sudden shout from the shore made them look up and take notice.

"I rather think they want us to row in," Tatler said, peering through the fog in the direction of the voice. Campbell hastily gulped down the remains of his coffee and replaced his flask in his rucksack before reaching for the oars. Fitting them back into the rowlocks took seconds and with a few sweeps of his arm, he deftly brought the boat round. It took only a few minutes of steady rowing before the wet, wooden columns of the jetty suddenly loomed, tall and dripping, out of the gloom.

"Ah, there you are, sirs," smiled a waiting boatman, catching the painter and winding it round a nearby bollard. "A pity the mist had to spoil your day."

Duncan, who had managed to catch two trout, dumped his gear on the jetty and as he took his catch to be weighed, the Chief Constable and George Tatler watched him speculatively.

Tatler looked at the policeman. "Well, Sir Archibald, do you believe our young friend's stories of monsters and dragons?"

The policeman's eyebrows rose a fraction as he realized that he'd been recognized. He looked shrewdly at Tatler and smiled slightly in acknowledgement. "If," he said, shaking his head, "if he hadn't mentioned the dragon and the transporter, I'd have said he was a bit of a lunatic ... but, as I said, I was on Arthur's Seat that night and it so happens that I can confirm at least one part of his story; for the transporter we stopped had two men and two children in the cab. Not only that, I recognized one of the men. He was at school with a cousin of mine."

Tatler nodded. "The long arm of coincidence," he said softly. "Strange how often it turns up in our line of work." He took one of his cards from an inside pocket and handed it to the Chief Constable. It was not a card that he gave to many people. "I'd be interested to see a copy of Mr Campbell's film and hear the results of your investigation, Chief Constable. Perhaps you would be kind enough to keep me informed?"

The Chief Constable raised his eyebrows as he read the card and his glance was searching as he looked at George Tatler speculatively and with a new respect.

"I will indeed, sir," he said.

2. Haggis and Oatcakes

Neil and Clara MacLean looked at one another in amazement as their mother put a very large haggis in the middle of the table. As this was the third time in two weeks that she had given them haggis, Neil opened his mouth to protest strongly but closed it again as Clara frowned and tilted her head warningly towards their guest. Complaints would have to be made later, for Mr MacGregor, the janitor at their school, was lunching with them that day.

"Let me serve you some haggis, Angus," Janet MacLean offered as she slit the skin with a knife and watched the steam rise as the haggis fell gently away. "John will be joining us in a minute. He's been on the hill all morning."

Angus MacGregor nodded understandingly. "Aye, it's not an easy job being a Park Ranger on Arthur's Seat with all the tourists around. He was telling me the other day that he's had to work a lot of overtime lately." He sat back in his chair and looked round the table. "I was hoping he might manage a game of darts this evening. It'd be like old times."

Neil grinned. "He'll be honoured, Mr MacGregor! It's not every day that he gets the chance to play the Scottish champion, after all!"

Angus MacGregor reddened. Although his rise to fame in the darts' world had made him a household name throughout Scotland, he hadn't let it go to his head. "Ach, it's not that way at all when your dad and I play — and fine you know it, young Neil."

"Clara," her mother smiled, "I can hear your dad in

the kitchen. Will you give him a hand to bring in the neeps and tatties."

"A grand meal, the haggis!" praised Mr MacGregor as generous spoonfuls were heaped onto his plate. "I was saying to my Maggie the other day that we ought to have it more often. There's nothing like good Scottish food!"

John MacLean overheard this last remark as he brought the mashed potatoes into the dining room, followed by Clara who carefully carried a steaming bowl of heavily-buttered, mashed turnips. "Strange that you should say that," he smiled, "I was reading in the paper just this morning that there has been a huge rise in the sale of haggis."

"Not only haggis," his wife remarked, passing the serving dishes round, "oatcakes, shortbread and Dundee cake as well. I bought a nice Dundee cake the other day from a shop in Princes Street. They had them on offer."

The mention of Princes Street made Neil frown. "Isn't Princes Street a bit much these days?" he queried. "I walked along it yesterday and the shop windows were totally over the top! Plastered in tartan!"

"It's actually very nice," his mother rejoined defensively, "very ... *tasteful*. And they've got tartan carpets inside as well, you know. Some shops have even hung banners in their windows showing the arms and insignia of all the clans. It really makes you feel proud to be Scottish."

"Aye," agreed Mr MacGregor, "Edinburgh is looking very nice indeed. Even the High Street is full of old flags — and have you noticed that a lot more men are wearing the kilt?"

"It's a real pity that women can't wear proper kilts," Janet MacLean mourned. "I was thinking of buying some tartan and having a long skirt made up."

"What's the matter with you, Mum?" Clara asked curiously. "You've never wanted to wear tartan before."

"Well, I know, but it's very fashionable these days. Everyone seems to be wearing it, haven't you noticed?"

Ranger MacLean frowned uneasily. He *had* noticed the sudden passion for tartan that seemed to have gripped the country and although it was undoubtedly good for tourism to have Scotland looking so uniquely Scottish, he objected to the plastic, tartan banners that now flapped from many government buildings.

"Actually, I was thinking of buying a kilt myself," confided Mr MacGregor to the table in general, "but I'm not sure that I have the figure for it."

Fortunately, at that precise moment, the MacLean's cat, Mischief, came meowing round the table so none of the adults noticed the broad grin that split Neil's face as he visualized the stocky figure of old MacGregor stomping up and down the playground in a kilt!

Clara also hid a grin as she slid from her chair and picked up the little cat.

"Goodness," said Mr MacGregor in amazement, "that's never the wee cat you took from the school, is it? My, she's come on grand! I told you she'd put on weight with your mother to feed her."

"Put her in the kitchen, Clara," her mother instructed with a smile, "and give her some fish from the fridge if she's hungry. She loves fish," she confessed, looking round the table. "I know it's expensive these days but the fishmonger slips me the odd bit for her now and then."

"Aye," MacGregor snorted, "it's all the fault of these foreign boats! They're out there every day, pinching our fish."

Janet MacLean nodded. "I saw the news this morning and it wasn't good. There seems to have been a real set-to last night between the Scottish and French fleets. A lot of nets were cut. It's really getting out of hand you know, and that Marcel Bruiton, the French Foreign Minister, seems to be positively egging them on."

"Well, if it goes on like this, it could develop into a fully-fledged war," her husband said with a slight frown. "Bruiton really seems to have it in for us. The East Coast fishermen are absolutely furious and the French fishing fleet is huge, you know. It outnumbers ours by at least three to one and, quite frankly, there's not a lot our lads can do if the French trawlers gang up on them."

"Can't the Scottish parliament do anything?" queried Neil.

His father shook his head. "I don't know, Neil. You'll have to ask Sir James when you see him next. Now that he's a Member of the Scottish Parliament, he'll be able to tell you the ins and outs of it all."

"Aye, he's a good man, that Sir James! He certainly talks a lot more sense than that other fellow that got elected," agreed Mr MacGregor.

"You mean the fellow with the long hair and fancy waistcoats — what's his name — Ned Stuart?" Janet MacLean frowned disapprovingly.

"Come on, Janet," excused the Ranger mildly, thinking back to the days of his youth, "Stuart's young and most youngsters tend to dress a bit exotically, don't they? From what I hear of him, he seems a pleasant enough chap."

"Aye, but age makes a difference," argued MacGregor, "and that Sir James has a much better head on his shoulders. I was reading one of his articles in *The*

Scotsman only the other day. I didn't know you knew him, though," he added, curiosity tingeing his voice.

Although MacGregor knew nothing of their remarkable adventures with Sir James, the owner of a local distillery, he had, nevertheless, been unwittingly involved in their brush with magic and magicians. Mrs MacLean frowned warningly at her husband and quickly changed the subject of the conversation, for although all memory of faeries and magic carpets had been wiped from MacGregor's mind, she was afraid that a chance word might recall his part in the adventure.

"You didn't tell us about your anniversary dinner, Angus," she remarked casually. "Maggie was telling me that you found a new Turkish restaurant in the High Street and went there."

"Aye, we did," he frowned at the memory.

"You don't sound very impressed," smiled the Ranger.

"Aye, well, there was nothing wrong with the food, you understand; we had a really good meal. I think it must have been the atmosphere of the place. It's down one of yon thin, dark passages near the old White Horse Inn. An odd place for a restaurant and," he struggled to express his feelings, "... it was very foreign."

"Well, you'd expect that of a Turkish restaurant, wouldn't you?" the Ranger remarked reasonably.

"Were there many people there?" queried Mrs MacLean. "A full restaurant's usually a sign of good food."

"Oh, aye, it was quite crowded and when I told the waiters it was our anniversary, they found us a good table and made us feel the most important people in the place! No one else got half the attention we did."

"That was nice," said Mrs MacLean, spooning more haggis onto his plate.

Mr MacGregor put his knife and fork down and pondered. "I wouldn't say that," he said slowly. "I wouldn't say that at all. They were all smiles with their turbans and incense but all the time ... it's stupid, I know ... but looking back on it, I realize that I felt uneasy the whole time I was there."

The Ranger sat back in his chair and regarded Angus MacGregor thoughtfully. He wasn't, the Ranger knew, the most imaginative of men and he wondered what had happened to cause him such disquiet. "Perhaps you should mention it to the local police and ask them to take a look," he suggested.

MacGregor snorted. "Aye, if they can find it!"

There was a slightly stunned silence as they eyed him in surprise.

"I tell you," he said defensively, "I was suspicious of the place and one lunch break I ... well, I walked over from the school to take a look at it in daylight." His voice sank dramatically and his accent broadened as he leant towards them. "Without a word of a lie, I'm tellin' ye, I walked up and down yon bit of the High Street ten times over and do you think I could find the entrance to the close? It was a narrow entrance, I admit, but I couldn't find it anywhere, and I haven't found it yet, even though I look for it every time I pass. It's no' there, I tell you. It's disappeared! Completely disappeared!"

3. Dance of the Dervishes

It was a dark night and raining hard. Although the street lamps threw streaks of flickering light over the wet pavements of the High Street, Neil felt a shiver of apprehension at a subtle darkening of the atmosphere that seemed to make the street narrower and the surrounding buildings taller, shabbier and more forbidding, as though they'd moved a hundred years back in time. He moved closer to Sir James and saw that Clara, walking under her mother's umbrella, was also looking apprehensive; her hand clutching at the firestone pendant she was wearing round her neck.

"Do you think we'll find the restaurant?" Neil whispered to Sir James. "Old MacGregor might have been exaggerating the whole thing. I mean, restaurants don't just disappear, do they?"

Sir James smiled at him, his eyes alert. "I wasn't sure when we started out but now ..." he scanned a street that seemed strangely deserted, "now I'm pretty sure we'll find it. There's magic abroad tonight, Neil! Can't you feel the change in the atmosphere? I'm not sure if your mother shouldn't take you both home and leave your dad and me to deal with this."

"No way!" Neil and Clara chorused. "We're in this together. Even Mum doesn't want to back out! Do you, Mum?"

Mrs MacLean shook her head, not quite knowing what all the fuss was about. "Of course not," she said. "I think it was a lovely idea to come here. Angus and Maggie said the food was excellent."

Neil looked at his mother sharply. Although she had been inside Arthur's Seat and had met the MacArthurs, the magic people who live in the hill, she hadn't been directly involved in their adventures and had never been given a firestone. Indeed, she had never needed one, but without a stone of her own she had no access to the world of magic that they enjoyed as a matter of course; for with their firestones they could call up magic carpets, become invisible and merge with people, birds and animals at will.

"Mum is the only one of us that isn't wearing a firestone," Neil said, meeting his father's eyes. "I think it makes a difference. She doesn't seem to feel what we're feeling."

Clara stopped suddenly beside a tall, narrow archway. Above their heads, an ornate, oriental lantern cast a dim light, illuminating a wooden plaque set in the stone wall.

"This must be it!" she whispered excitedly. "The restaurant *does* exist! What does the writing say, Neil?"

Her brother moved forward and looked at the flowing red script. *"The Sultan's Palace,"* he whispered.

"Shall ... shall we go down?" Clara questioned nervously, glancing down the alley that ran between high walls. At a nod from Sir James, she walked under the arch and even as she did so, she knew beyond doubt that this was a magic place. Excitement coursed through her veins and she felt the firestone hang suddenly heavy round her neck. Neil, too, drew in his breath with a gasp as he followed her through the arched way that gave onto a dank, narrow passage that sloped steeply before them. It was very quiet; the only sound being the steady drip of the rain. Wet cobbles gleamed dully and the high walls that seemed to meet overhead in the gloom, gave the place an air of mystery and romance.

Gripped by a strange exhilaration, they felt as though they had stepped suddenly from the ordinary world into the pages of an exotic adventure story.

In the distance, lit by a sudden shaft of light that streamed from an open door, they saw that the passage opened out into a sizeable courtyard and, as they watched, the figure of a man clad in a turban and flowing silk robes appeared in the doorway. He saw them immediately and paused, still as a statue.

Sir James eyed the Ranger. "What do you think?" he asked. "Shall we go on?"

It was Mrs MacLean who made the decision for them. Completely unaware of their misgivings, she sailed blithely down the alley, disturbing some pigeons that rose into the air, flapping in alarm, as she made her way towards the restaurant where the still, watchful figure of the Turk awaited them.

"Hang on, Mum!" Clara called, running after her. "Wait for us!"

As Mrs MacLean stopped and turned towards her, the Turk moved forward solicitously.

"Please be careful, Miss," he warned Clara. "The cobbles are a wee bit slippery with the rain. We don't want any broken legs, do we?"

All thoughts of magic promptly fled. The man was no more Turkish than they were. His accent was pure Edinburgh and now that they were nearer they could see that the silken robes that had looked so splendid and romantic from a distance, were actually creased and rather tawdry. Indeed, the restaurant now looked disappointingly ordinary, despite the whiff of incense that drifted from the ornate brass burners that lay inside the curtained doorway.

The waiter stepped forward, grinning at them cheerfully and with a polite bow, he gestured towards the entrance. "Welcome," he intoned, "to the *Sultan's Palace!*" And ushering them through a deeply-carpeted, dimly-lit foyer, led them into the restaurant itself.

As the restaurant doors closed behind the little party with a decisive click, the two pigeons that Mrs MacLean had disturbed, sailed down to the cobbles.

"That's torn it," snapped one. "They've gone in!"

"We couldn't have stopped them, Jaikie! Not without showing the Turks that we were watching the place."

"I know, I know, but this is serious, for goodness sake!" Jaikie flapped his wings in frustration. "Look, you'd better fly back to the hill and tell the MacArthur what's happened. I'll hang on here, just in case. Go on! Get moving!"

"Right, I'm off!" nodded the other and with a clap of wings, the pigeon soared skywards, heading towards the dark, misty bulk of Arthur's Seat; the hill set in the middle of Edinburgh that looks for all the world like a sleeping dragon.

Jaikie watched him go and then turned once again to the restaurant. He eyed it anxiously, his mind taken up by the sudden, totally unexpected, appearance of Sir James and the Park Ranger. How they had got wind of the Turks he had no idea, but to take Clara and Neil into such danger defied belief. He groaned inwardly as he realized just how much they had complicated matters; the MacArthur was going to have a fit when he heard the news!

While Jaikie sat outside the restaurant, trying hard not to panic, Sir James and the Ranger were looking round the inside with interest as they made their way through chattering groups of diners, to their table. The decor was opulently rich; a dazzle of ornate gold wallpaper, red velvet curtains and crystal chandeliers. By far the most striking feature of the room, however, was an assortment of tall mirrors. Set in heavy, iron frames decorated with birds and flowers, they stretched along the walls from floor to ceiling, reflecting the white table linen and the sparkling glitter of candles and crystal.

At one end of the room, a band of musicians played on a raised stage, while a tall woman, dressed in flowing purple satin, sang into a microphone. Behind her, a backcloth depicted a rather garishly-painted country scene, so crudely done that it looked like the work of children. Its bright, blue sky framed a road overhung by trees that seemed to lead to a distant castle while, in the foreground, a village of thatched, peasant cottages lay in lush, green meadows dotted with improbably-coloured flowers.

Neil looked at the band with interest as many of the instruments were unfamiliar to him. Violins and flutes, he recognized, but they were mixed with strange hand drums, long penny whistles and what he thought might be zithers. Clara, however, more interested in the musicians than their instruments, thought them a decidedly fearsome lot.

"They look more like bandits than musicians," she confided to Sir James as he unfolded his napkin and reached for the menu.

Sir James was inclined to agree. They were certainly colourful. The men wore baggy trousers, flowing red tunics and jewelled turbans, but it didn't take any great flight of the imagination to visualize them clutching rifles or even barbaric scimitars. However, they certainly knew how to play and the music, although strangely discordant, had a haunting charm of its own.

Sir James did the ordering and the table was soon overflowing with a variety of dishes that tasted delicious. The waiters hovered attentively, helping them to spicy kebabs, stuffed vine leaves and roasted aubergine dips.

Finally, they could eat no more. "That was a truly delicious meal," Mrs MacLean said, patting her lips with the napkin as the waiters removed their plates.

"Mmm," agreed her husband, "I ate far too much!"

They sat back in their chairs, relaxed and happy. Clara sighed as a feeling of complete contentment stole over her. The music seemed to be sending her into a gentle dream, or perhaps, she thought, it was the drift of incense that wafted over their table from the smouldering coals in the iron braziers that now burned with peculiar, greenish flames.

Idly she looked at the garish backcloth at the back of the little stage and wondered how she could ever have thought it tacky. It now seemed incredibly beautiful and even as she gazed at it, a strange longing rose within her. The blue sky and green trees behind the cottage spoke of lazy summer days, and the road that led to the castle promised a new world of adventure, magic and excitement.

Suddenly, the restaurant's lights darkened, spotlights blazed on the stage and the music shrieked to a piercing crescendo as, into their dazzling brightness, leapt a group of strangely-clad young men wearing the red fez of the Turk. Their baggy trousers were covered by long white dresses whose finely-pleated skirts started to billow out as they circled the stage, whirling like spinning tops. As the music quickened, so the dancers whirled faster and faster until they became a moving blur of white that held the audience dazzled and enthralled.

How long the dance lasted they never knew but as the incense in the braziers flared fiery red and its magic seeped insidiously through the room, the dancers

beckoned them forward. Lured by the unseen forces
that now captivated them, the Ranger and Sir James
rose from their chairs and started to walk, as though in
a dream, towards the stage. Clara followed and found
herself pulling at Neil's hand in her eagerness to reach
the painted village that promised such untold delights.
Mrs MacLean, startled at their sudden departure,
picked up her handbag and tripped anxiously behind,
not quite sure what was happening.

The music rose to an eerie climax as, on reaching the
painted doorway of the rustic peasant's hut, Sir James
and the Ranger bent their heads and followed the dancers unhesitatingly into the gloom beyond. Neil and
Clara followed them in but Mrs MacLean hung back in
sudden horror as she realized that the door to the cottage was not really a door at all. It was a huge mirror
similar to those that lined the walls of the restaurant
and even as Clara walked through it, the dim interior
of the cottage vanished abruptly, leaving Mrs MacLean
staring horrified at her own reflection.

4. The French Connection

Count Louis de Charillon, the French Consul in Edinburgh, turned up the collar of his coat against the rain and looked at the taxi in distaste as he paid off the driver. Like so many of the taxis and buses in Edinburgh these days, it was painted in a particularly vicious-looking tartan that did much to offend his sensibilities.

He pursed his lips and shook his head slightly. What *was* it with the Scots these days that made them parade themselves, and their city, in tartan? Princes Street was awash in it and George Street ... he shuddered at the memory of the dreadful banners that looped the street. Thank goodness, he thought, as he looked searchingly up and down, that the craze hadn't yet reached the refined elegance of Moray Place, whose Georgian façade swept before him in a gracious curve. Pocketing his change as the tartan monstrosity drove off, he turned and mounted the shallow steps that led to the door of an imposing town house, scattering a couple of pigeons as he did so. Even as he raised his hand to the knocker, however, the door swung open and a fair-haired young man greeted him warmly.

"Monsieur le Comte! Welcome!"

"Mr Stuart, how are you?" Monsieur le Comte de Charillon entered the tiled hall and shook hands with his host as the butler closed the great door against the wind and driving rain.

The two pigeons, fluttering back down to resume their vigil on a stretch of railings beside the house, fluffed their feathers against the cold and eyed one another speculatively as the door closed.

"Monsieur le Comte?" repeated one. "Now, that's interesting!"

"It's French," contributed the other.

Hamish regarded Archie sourly. "I know it's French," he said irritably, shifting on his claws. "But why would Kalman be entertaining a Frenchman? That's what I want to know. Aren't we supposed to be at loggerheads with the French these days?"

"*And* he called Prince Kalman, 'Mr Stuart'," added Archie. "Let's hope the MacArthur can work that one out!"

Hamish nodded. "It's a pity the prince has put a protective shield round his house," he mourned, looking longingly at the curtained windows. "I'd give my eye teeth to hear what's being said in there."

"Pigeons don't have eye teeth," Archie grinned and promptly wilted under Hamish's look of scorn. "Sorry," he muttered. "Just a joke!"

"Will you try to remember that this is a serious mission," hissed Hamish, "and give it some attention! We've been hanging round here for days and this is the first time we've managed to pick up anything at all valuable."

"Can we go back to the hill, then and tell the MacArthur?" asked Archie hopefully. "I'm frozen solid."

"No, no, we'd better not," Hamish said thoughtfully. "We'll wait here and follow this Frenchman home. The MacArthur will want to know who he is and where he lives."

"Aye, I suppose you're right," Archie admitted gloomily and as raindrops dripped off his wings, prepared for a long, cold wait.

Inside the house, however, the count paused and relaxed gratefully in the warmth that washed over him.

"Come this way, my dear Louis," Stuart murmured as the butler relieved his visitor of gloves and overcoat. "There are only the two of us, I'm afraid. I do hope you don't mind being entertained in my study?" He pushed open the study door and gestured to his visitor to enter. "But don't despair! I've a special treat for you this evening; a new addition to my collection that I think will interest you."

A blazing fire crackled in a handsome marble fireplace and as de Charillon warmed his hands gratefully at the leaping flames, he glanced round the room appreciatively. Its walls were lined with old books, mahogany gleamed and the comfortably upholstered armchairs beside the fire were reflected in two tall, strangely-framed mirrors that lay on either side of a heavily-curtained window.

Stuart gestured to one of the chairs. "Do sit down," he murmured.

Louis de Charillon sat and regarded his host thoughtfully. As French Consul, he represented the interests of France in Scotland and well aware that diplomatic relations between the two countries were at an all time low because of the dispute over North Sea fishing rights, wondered why he had been asked to come. Not that it was at all unusual for him to be invited. He had, in actual fact, been a guest in the house many times before as Edward, or "Ned," Stuart, a Member of the Scottish Parliament, entertained frequently.

The butler brought in refreshments and once the door closed behind him, Stuart, as the count had expected, got down to the serious business of the battle of the trawlers. De Charillon shifted uneasily in his chair for he had serious personal doubts as to the wisdom of his Foreign Minister's policy towards Britain

and knew perfectly well that in many places his arguments stood on extremely shaky ground.

Stuart knew it, too. "Your arguments, my dear
Louis, just don't hold water. The truth is that your
trawlers are fishing illegally and you know it!" He
raised his hand as the count sat up abruptly, his face
set in lines of anger at such un-diplomatic plain speaking.

Edward Stuart smiled. "It strikes me that what you
stand in need of in Scotland just now is a ... friend, shall
we say? An ... influential friend?"

It says much for the count's training that he did not
betray, by even the flicker of an eyelash, that he was
shocked to the core. He had certainly not expected this,
and his eyes hardened as he regarded the handsome
face that looked at him so steadily. There was a long
pause before he spoke. "And you, my dear Edward ... do
you propose to be this *influential* friend?" he queried.

"That," Ned Stuart smiled, "is something we might
discuss later. First of all, I have some papers that I
would like you to have a look at."

He rose to his feet and the count noted that for someone so generally self-possessed, he seemed strangely
excited. As he moved towards a massive desk, scattered
with papers, he adjusted a cloth that covered a bulky
object on a small side table.

"The new addition to your collection, Ned?" the
count hazarded a guess.

"Yes! Yes, it is. But I'm not going to show it to you
just yet. I wonder if you would like to give me your
opinion of these papers? They arrived only last night
so I haven't had time to assess them properly, and too
excited, I might add. I've been on their trail for a very
long time and can't believe," he stepped to one side as
the count rose and moved to his side, "... the truth is

that I still can't believe that I managed to trace them," he continued. "They're in French, as you see. Be careful, won't you; the paper is quite fragile ..."

De Charillon, intrigued at the nervousness in Stuart's voice, sat at the desk and pulling up a chair, drew the rolls of yellowed documents carefully towards him. As he scanned the first page, however, his casual manner deserted him and his body stiffened.

"But this is amazing ..." he muttered, sitting up abruptly and casting his host a look of complete and utter astonishment.

Stuart, perched on the edge of the desk, nodded silently and continued to watch tensely as, turning once more to the documents, the count proceeded to read each page very thoroughly indeed.

"My dear Edward," he said weakly, looking up at last. "These papers," he gestured towards them, "seem to ... seem to imply that you are a direct descendant of Charles Edward Stuart!"

"Bonnie Prince Charlie!" nodded Stuart. He heaved a sigh and frowned thoughtfully. "If the Jacobite Rebellion hadn't failed, he would have been king of both England and Scotland, you know. My father long suspected that we were descended from him but we never had the proof. Until now, that is."

"But if they ..." the count gestured towards the collection of letters and birth certificates, "... *if* they are genuine, they certainly make you a high-ranking nobleman of Scotland. A prince, perhaps."

"Certainly, a prince," Stuart smiled confidently. "If, that is, your French archivists testify to the authenticity of the papers."

The two men looked at one another in silence and again Stuart smiled as understanding dawned in the eyes of the Frenchman.

"You *do* see that French recognition of my title would strengthen my case immeasurably, don't you?" he murmured.

As de Charillon nodded, Stuart said softy. "You see, I don't only have the papers. I also have this!" And, with a flick of his wrist, he whisked off the cloth that covered the object on the table.

It was a crown; a spiked, iron crown set about with magnificent rubies. Had Sir James been present, he would have recognized it instantly; for it was a magic crown that had, in times past, belonged to the Sultan of Turkey. Stuart picked it up and held it reverently in both hands.

"The ancient crown of the Scots!" he lied glibly.

The count stood transfixed. He was not a fool and looking at the man with the crown in his hands told him all he wanted to know. Ned Stuart did not just want to be a prince: he wanted to be King of Scotland!

5. Rothlan Takes Charge

Although Mrs MacLean stood aghast, staring in shocked horror at her reflection in the mirror she, nevertheless, understood immediately what had happened. Stretching out her hand, she touched the glass tentatively. It was hard and unyielding. No way was she going to be able to get through it. It must, she thought, be a magic mirror. Yes, that was it — it was a magic mirror and it probably hadn't let her through because she wasn't wearing a firestone. She frowned. *Now* what was she going to do?

She swung round as a sudden flash of light crackled out of nowhere and such was its force that she almost fell to the floor. The noise, however, heralded the arrival of another player on the stage; for facing the motley group of Turks that had surged towards her, stood a tall, slim stranger dressed in a kilt and velvet jacket. It was the fearsome eagle perched on his shoulder that gave Mrs MacLean the clue to his identity and she sighed with relief as she realized that the man who had appeared so suddenly out of the blue, must be Lord Rothlan.

She looked at him in amazement. Was this really the fantastic magician that Neil had talked about nonstop? Her husband had been full of praise for him and Clara had often told her how much she adored the eagle. Amgarad, that's what she had called it. She had no idea how Lord Rothlan and Amgarad had arrived but now that they had appeared on the scene, she knew she was in safe hands.

"You must be Mrs MacLean," the stranger said in a pleasant voice as she turned towards him. "Let me introduce myself," he said with a bow. "My name is Alasdair Rothlan."

"Yes, I thought you must be," Mrs MacLean smiled as she met the warm, brown eyes of the handsome young man who stood before her. "I'm Janet MacLean, Neil and Clara's mother. I ... I don't quite know what happened here, but I'm more than glad to see you." Her eyes turned to the eagle that rested on his shoulder. "And ... is this Amgarad? That Clara loves so much?"

The great eagle bent its head in welcome but at a sudden movement, its eyes suddenly shifted from Mrs MacLean to the Turks behind her and as several of them moved forward, he flapped his wings warningly. Moving closer to Lord Rothlan, she watched them approach and grasped his arm anxiously.

"These people," she gestured towards the Turks, "have taken Sir James and my husband and children through that mirror."

"Yes, I saw them," Rothlan answered, looking at the Turks sternly. "I watched them through my crystal. This mirror, did you say?"

Lord Rothlan turned to the mirror that formed the cottage door. Moving forward, he ran his hands delicately over the ornate, iron frame, decorated with carvings of flowers and animals, and let his hand rest gently on a carved rose.

"No!" one of the Turks ran up warningly. "Don't turn it, milord! Don't turn it or we will be lost. Please, milord, the time-frame is set!"

"And where would it take me if I were to step through?" Rothlan asked evenly.

"Milord, to the Sultan's Palace!"

Even as the Turk answered, however, the mirror rippled suddenly and a tall, imposing figure stepped through it. Rothlan recognized him immediately. The Sultan of Turkey himself, no less! He drew Mrs MacLean back as the Sultan was followed by an entourage of equally exotic figures that piled and scrambled into the room after him. Dressed in robes of turquoise and gold and wearing a turban strung with ropes of pearls, the bearded, hawk-like face of the Sultan regarded Lord Rothlan grimly.

"I think it's time that you and I had words, Rothlan," he snapped. "You've been up to mischief and I want to know why!"

Rothlan bowed low. "Your Majesty!" he murmured.

The Sultan inclined his head.

"Make your bow, Mrs MacLean," Lord Rothlan said, smiling slightly. "This is His Majesty, the Sultan of Turkey, Sultan Sulaiman the Red."

As Mrs MacLean curtseyed awkwardly, all the people in the restaurant threw themselves on the ground, prostrating themselves before their ruler. The Sultan waved his hand in casual recognition of their presence and after a swift, rather disdainful glance round the restaurant, gestured impatiently towards the mirror.

"I think you will find my palace a lot more comfortable than this," he said commandingly. "Shall we go?"

It was an order rather than a request and given the charged atmosphere and the threatening growl from the Turks, Lord Rothlan thought it wise to comply. He nodded assent and turned to Mrs MacLean.

"Don't worry, Mrs MacLean," he said reassuringly, "you'll see the others shortly. We've got to go through the mirror, though. Take my hand and we'll be able to go through it together."

"But where will it take us?" asked Mrs MacLean.

"Why to the Sultan's Palace," Rothlan answered, "where else?"

"But isn't this ... I thought ... this restaurant is the *Sultan's Palace,* isn't it?"

"Ah!" smiled Rothlan. "But we are going to his real palace ... in Turkey!"

"In Turkey!" Although Mrs MacLean's eyes widened at the thought, she was not without courage and her hand unhesitatingly grasped Rothlan's as, with Amgarad on his shoulder, he followed the Sultan through the magic mirror.

Jaikie, sitting hunched against the pouring rain in the branches of one of the ornamental trees in the little courtyard outside, sat up, alert and anxious, as he heard a dull rumble of sound from inside the restaurant. He knew immediately what it meant and with more speed than grace, shot straight up into the air in a fair imitation of a rocket.

He was just in time. Perching precariously on the edge of an old chimney stack, he peered down into the narrow passageway below and watched in horror as the vennel, the little courtyard and the restaurant, slowly fragmented and with a last, tantalizing ripple, disappeared before his eyes — with Sir James and the MacLeans still inside!

Totally devastated, he shivered at the enormity of it all. The MacArthur was most certainly going to tear strips off him for this!

6. The Sultan's Palace

The wall-to-wall heat hit Mrs MacLean in a comfortable wave as she stepped through the mirror and opened her eyes to a magical scene of blue skies, blazing sun, green palm trees and the sweeping curve of white marble pillars that encircled the high terrace of the Sultan's palace.

"Mum!" Neil and Clara, who had turned at the sudden arrival of the Sultan, were amazed to see their mother step through the magic mirror after him, still clutching Lord Rothlan's hand. Sir James and the Ranger, who had been lounging idly on gaudily-covered silk divans, jumped to their feet and advanced on Rothlan and Mrs MacLean in some relief. Amgarad, however, flew immediately to Clara and perched on her shoulder making delighted shrieking noises.

"Amgarad!" exclaimed Clara happily, "it's so nice to see you again. I've really missed you!"

"I've missed you, too, Clara," the bird said in his deep, croaky voice, rubbing his head against her cheek. "It's a long time since you last visited Jarishan."

Although they had tried, neither Neil nor Clara had ever been able to work out how they managed to understand Amgarad, for he certainly wasn't speaking English as such, but somehow his eagle noises seemed to form words that they could hear in their heads.

With the eagle still on her shoulder, Clara ran to her mother and took her hand. Words tumbled out of her. "Mum, I'm so happy you're here! This is a fabulous place and the Sultan has been so kind to us. And this," she said excitedly, "*this* is Amgarad!"

She broke off as the Sultan clapped his hands and ushered them all, politely but firmly, towards the divans. At his signal, servants dressed in flowing white robes appeared from arched doorways, carrying trays of sliced fruit, cakes and pastries and jugs of fruit juice, tinkling with ice. Mrs MacLean sat bemused as they passed the food around and watched in horror as her husband piled his plate with a selection of sticky pastries.

"How can you, John?" she questioned. "You've just eaten the most enormous meal!"

"I've what?" he looked startled.

"The meal at the restaurant. Aren't you still full?"

"But," the Ranger looked at her oddly, "that was last week ..."

"Last week!" she repeated incredulously. "But ... you only finished eating about ten minutes ago!"

"I think," interrupted Lord Rothlan soothingly, "you will find that time is different here. I wouldn't worry about it; just relax and enjoy yourselves. The Sultan is a wonderful host."

"Do you know him, Lord Rothlan?" whispered Mrs MacLean. "He seemed to know you."

"I've known him for a long time," Rothlan said seriously, "although this is the first time I've seen him in years. In the old days, you know, Turkey made the best magic carpets in the world. Everyone came here to buy them."

"Before Prince Kalman's father stole the crown," Neil observed quietly.

Rothlan nodded. "Prince Casimir! Yes, the Sultan was so furious at losing the crown, and most of his power with it, that he hasn't spoken to anyone in Scotland since!"

"How did Kalman's father, this Prince Casimir, manage to steal the crown?" Mrs MacLean asked curiously.

Rothlan pursed his lips and frowned. "Casimir," he sighed, "was always proud and could be a bit arrogant, but underneath it all he was a pleasant enough chap really. Perhaps some strange magic influenced him, I don't know — but the fact remains that while he was visiting Turkey one summer, he seemed to change completely and become totally and utterly obsessed by the crown."

"Wasn't that a bit crazy?" queried Neil. "After all, it wasn't any old crown, was it? It was the Sultan's crown."

Rothlan smiled in agreement. "Exactly, Neil. He couldn't buy it, for it wasn't for sale and he couldn't steal it as it was too well guarded, so he tricked the Sultan into staging a contest with the crown as the prize. No one expected the Sultan to lose, of course, but lose he did and he had to hand the crown over of his own free will. It was only when Casimir was on his way back to Scotland on his magic carpet that the Sultan realized that he'd cheated. Needless to say, he was furious and sent the storm carriers after him to get the crown back."

"But they didn't get it back, Mum," Neil said, turning to his mother. "Casimir threw it off the carpet and that's when it fell into Lord Rothlan's loch at Jarishan."

Overhearing his words, Clara felt a creeping sense of unease. She looked anxiously at the Sultan who no longer seemed the kindly host she knew. Now frowningly stern and abrupt, his eyes were angry and his lips set in a tight, thin line.

It wasn't until they'd finished eating and the food had been removed that the conversation took a serious turn. Clara listened with a sinking heart as the Sultan brought up the subject of the stolen crown.

"You made a big mistake in calling up the storm carriers to defend Jarishan last year, Rothlan! They sensed the crown was in your loch from the minute they arrived. Did you think that they wouldn't?"

Lord Rothlan looked at him quizzically. "So you think *I* have it, your majesty?"

"Now that we've met, Rothlan," the Sultan retorted sourly, "I know that you *don't*. But I've good reason to believe that the MacArthur might, for the storm carriers saw him and his army in the hills round Jarishan last year. That's why I sent my people to Edinburgh. To search for it."

Rothlan frowned. "The storm carriers weren't mistaken, but you must believe me, your majesty, when I say that the MacArthur doesn't have the crown."

"Then why did he put a protective shield round Arthur's Seat, the minute he found out we were in Edinburgh?"

"Your majesty, you must forgive him, but surely under the circumstances it was understandable?" Rothlan's glance was almost indignant. "After all, you haven't spoken to any of us in years!"

The Sultan glowered threateningly. "If what you say is true and the MacArthur *doesn't* have the crown, then who has?" he demanded. "Tell me!"

Rothlan looked at him consideringly for a moment and sat back, stifling a sigh. "You're not going to like this," he said evenly, "but I rather think Prince Kalman has it!"

The Sultan, his face pale with fury, leapt to his feet and strode up and down in anger. "*Kalman!*" he hissed venomously. "Kalman Meriden! Casimir's son! When I get my hands on him I'll tear him to pieces!"

Rothlan gave a wry smile. "If he has the crown that will be difficult, your majesty, for its magic will guard him."

The Sultan grunted in annoyance at the truth of this and, in a swirl of silken robes, flung himself down on a divan. Adjusting a few cushions, he pulled up his feet and sat cross-legged. "You'd better tell me the story from the beginning, Rothlan," he snapped. "And don't miss *anything* out!"

Alasdair Rothlan smiled wryly and, choosing his words carefully, told the Sultan what he knew. "Rumour," he began, "has always had it that the crown fell from the carpet before the storm carriers killed Casimir," he said. "Needless to say, Kalman scoured the area but although the remains of his carpet were found, his father's body was never recovered. Nor, of course, was the crown." He shrugged. "It was only recently, when he had the idea of having his father's carpet sewn back together, that he started searching again. You see, he made it tell him everything that happened that night."

"Did he, indeed," muttered the Sultan, looking at Rothlan searchingly.

Rothlan nodded. "Before he died, Casimir apparently turned the crown's magic in on itself and tied it to the Meriden family forever. It must have fought against the hex, though, for when he threw the crown off the carpet, it didn't land in Ardray as he'd planned, but fell into my loch instead." He looked thoughtful. "But the fact remains," he said slowly, a shade of puzzlement crossing his face, "that although it must have lain there for many years, it still hid itself from me."

"That's a good point" the Sultan said, meeting his eyes. "I also wonder why that was."

Rothlan shrugged and continued his tale. As the story progressed and he outlined everything that had happened in Jarishan the previous year, the Sultan, to Clara's relief, seemed to relax and by the end of the story, looked more concerned than angry.

"So the children were never directly involved with the crown?" he said. "They weren't in the loch with you?"

Rothlan shook his head. "Neil was still suffering from *dragonsleep* and we wouldn't let either Ellan or Clara in the loch. It was too dangerous."

Neil and Clara blinked as the Sultan turned towards them, his look suddenly becoming searching and penetrating. For an instant, they felt a power stronger than anything they had ever experienced, surge through their minds. "Wow," Clara gasped, looking at the Sultan in astonishment, "how did you do that?"

But he only smiled in answer and, to her relief, was once more the kind Sultan that she knew and liked. Nevertheless, the memory of his anger stayed with her and she shivered as she thought of Prince Kalman's fate should he ever be at his mercy.

"If what you say is true, Rothlan, and he does have the crown, then he's very powerful and an enemy to be feared. Make no mistake, he's every bit as cunning as his father was before him! We, therefore, must be clever, too. Clever *and* cunning."

No one dared to speak as, lounging back against the cushions, he stroked his beard.

"There may be a way, though," he said, pursing his lips thoughtfully. "As you know, we, the Osmanli, have always owned the crown and know many of its secrets. Without it my magic, as you know, has been severely weakened over the years but you, Alasdair, are a powerful magician. If you speak truly and are willing to help me, then it is possible that together we could take the crown from the prince."

"I am more than willing to help you, your majesty," Rothlan answered immediately, "and I'm sure the MacArthur will, too, once he knows the situation. He's been helping me look for the prince for some time now and he knows just as well as I do that in Kalman's hands, the crown is a threat to us all."

"Then," the Sultan announced, rising to his feet, "I suggest that tomorrow we go to Scotland to visit the MacArthur. He has mirrors, does he not?"

7. Mirror, Mirror on the Wall

"Arthur! Arthur! Wake up!"

At the sound of Archie's voice, the great dragon rolled over on his bed of treasure, settled himself comfortably and covered both ears with his wings.

"Arthur, *will* you wake up!"

Arthur rolled over again in the hope that Archie would go away. He hadn't finished his afternoon nap and was in the middle of a particularly exciting dream involving deep, dark forests, knights and castles.

"Wake – up – Arthur!" shouted Archie. "Come on, I know you're awake!"

Irritably, the dragon slowly opened his wonderful eyes and looked at the small, sheepskin-clad figure that was shaking him out of his dream.

"Go away, Archie. I want to sleep!" he muttered and made to close his eyes again when Archie gave him a tremendous thump that although it didn't hurt him, was enough to tell Arthur that something really was up.

"Arthur! For goodness sake, wake up! Something dreadful's happened!" Archie spoke rapidly as he shinned up on his back. "The Turks we've been watching in the High Street have somehow managed to get hold of Sir James and the MacLeans! It's awful! Jaikie's going frantic!"

"Not Neil and Clara as well?" Arthur sounded shocked.

"That's what he said! How they managed to get tangled up in all this, heaven alone knows," Archie gasped, getting a firm grip on Arthur's scales.

Arthur didn't hesitate. Now wide awake, he slithered his ungainly way down the huge pile of treasure, scattering gold and jewels as he went, and sped through the tunnels that led to the Great Hall at a speed that left Archie clinging to his neck for dear life. When they reached the huge cavern, they found it full of little people, clustered anxiously round a raised dais where a wizened old man sat on a large, carved chair. Dressed in boots, breeches and a long, somewhat tattered, sheepskin jacket draped haphazardly over a dull-red tunic, this was the MacArthur, chieftain of the magic people who live in the hill.

From his perch on the dragon's back, Archie stared across the hall for in front of the MacArthur glowed a delicate crystal ball that was, at that moment, pulsing with vibrant light. Archie promptly dug his heels into Arthur's flank and urged him forward.

The MacArthurs, who had been standing transfixed at the sight of the shining crystal, now scattered frantically as the dragon more or less screeched its way through them and came to a jarring halt. Miraculously, Archie managed to keep his seat and scrambling off the dragon's back, ran to Hamish and Jaikie who, with the MacArthur and his daughter, Lady Ellan, were gazing into the depths of the crystal.

The MacArthur smiled as Archie and Arthur joined them and repeated some instructions to Hamish, who was taking careful notes on a piece of paper. Archie sighed with relief as he heard Lord Rothlan assure the MacArthur that Sir James and the MacLeans were perfectly all right. However, even as he leant forward to get a better view, Rothlan bade them farewell and the light faded.

Hamish, totally absorbed, scanned the piece of paper he'd been writing on, made a few alterations to his notes and handed the sheet to the MacArthur, who took it carefully and bent over it, frowning short-sightedly as he fished in his pocket for his glasses.

"What on earth's going on?" Archie asked in amazement. "That was Rothlan's voice, wasn't it?"

Ignoring his question, Hamish turned to him with a sigh of relief. "Thank goodness you're here, Archie," he muttered, grasping his arm anxiously as he spoke. "Do you remember how to set the magic mirrors? It's really important as it's been ages since anyone's used them. Rothlan's given us instructions but they have to be absolutely spot-on accurate. It won't do to send the Sultan to Inner Mongolia or Mandarin China for that matter!"

"The what? To where?" Archie looked absolutely blank.

"Don't confuse Archie any more than you have to," Lady Ellan admonished, flapping an exasperated hand at Hamish. "Things are complicated enough without you rabbiting on about China!"

"Listen," she explained to Archie, who was looking more bewildered by the minute, "Alasdair ... Lord Rothlan ... has just contacted us from Turkey."

"Not China?" queried Archie.

"Forget China!" she said, "China has nothing to do with it!"

"But, Hamish ... "

"Listen to me, will you," her voice became impatient, "Sir James and the others are safe in Turkey and Alasdair wants to bring them back here through the mirrors and," she said, running her hands distractedly through her long, fair hair, "you're never going to believe this! The Sultan of Turkey is coming as well — with his entourage!"

"The Sultan of Turkey!" Archie and Arthur looked at one another in amazement. "You mean," Archie gulped, "that ...that Sulaiman the Red is coming here? To the hill?"

"Through the mirrors," she nodded, "and how we are going to cope with them all, I don't know. I doubt if we have enough bedrooms for a start; even in the old days he never travelled with less than fifty people!" She looked harassed and turning towards him, touched her father's arm. "Excuse me, won't you, father. I've a good bit of organizing to do if we are going to show our guests some good, Scottish hospitality!"

The MacArthur, who had finished reading the sheet Hamish had given him, took his glasses off and absently nodded his head. As his daughter headed purposefully for the kitchens, he turned to them in relief and patted Arthur absent-mindedly as the dragon, curled excitedly beside his great chair, puffed clouds of smoke that set them all coughing.

"Well, I don't know how Rothlan's done it," the MacArthur said, waving his hands around to disperse the haze, "but he certainly seems to have worked miracles! He's not only managed to mend fences with Sulaiman the Red but has rescued Sir James and the MacLeans as well. I don't mind telling you that Jaikie had me seriously worried when he told me the restaurant had disintegrated!"

"That's nothing to how *I* felt," Jaikie said, feelingly. He shook his head in disbelief. "How they ever found out about the Turks is a mystery! We'd barely found out about them ourselves!"

"We'll doubtless hear their side of the story when they arrive," soothed the MacArthur. "To tell you the truth, I still can't quite believe it! Sulaiman the Red — coming here in person! After all these years!"

"It's just as well he *is* coming, MacArthur," interrupted Archie. "Especially now that we know Prince

Kalman is in town. In fact, the sooner we start getting things organized the better."

The MacArthur nodded. "All the mirrors will have to be taken out of storage and set accurately for a start. Arthur will give you a hand with them."

"And another thing," Hamish added as Arthur flapped his wings, "what are we going to do about the shield we have in place round the hill? We can't afford to leave ourselves open and unprotected for very long, not with the prince around — and if Kitor, that crow of his, has been snooping about the place, well ..."

The MacArthur nodded. "You're right," he agreed, "it'll all have to be done pretty quickly. Otherwise you never know who might end up stepping through the mirrors."

8. The Tartan City

Several days after his conversation on the misty shores of Loch Leven with the Chief Constable of Edinburgh, George Tatler walked into King's Cross station in London, chatting idly with his secretary. As he often travelled to Scotland, he knew King's Cross well and his glance was therefore casual as it swept the broad expanse of the main concourse. His expression, however, quickly changed to one of concern as he approached his platform. He stared, totally thunderstruck at the sight that met his eyes, for its entire length was looped, hung and strung in tartan.

"What the devil's going on, Martin?" he queried, lifting his eyebrows in amazement at the sight of hordes of tartan-clad passengers. True, there were a few men in suits, but they were totally outnumbered by those in kilts. And the women! His eyes goggled at the long tartan skirts, ruffled blouses and vast, trailing, loose shawls that drifted around them. Even the children sported mini kilts and the theme seemed to have spilled over into tartan luggage, pushchairs and even the odd carrier bag.

"I told you it was bad," his secretary glanced at him apprehensively. "Edinburgh is a nightmare! Believe me, an absolute nightmare!"

"Good grief!" Tatler exclaimed. It was totally mind-boggling! He eyed the engines and carriages of the Intercity train with complete and utter horror as it pulled into the station. "I don't believe it," he said, stopping dead in his tracks as his eyes took in the full enormity of a train plastered from end to end in tartan.

"What's the matter with the Scots? Have they all gone mad?"

"That's as good an explanation as any," Martin said sourly. "They seem to be a law unto themselves these days. Just look at them!" he flapped his hand at the sea of Scottish passengers surging along the platform. "Tartan to the eyeballs!" He shook his head. "The real problem, as I see it, is that they don't seem to realize how totally over-the-top it all is! *They* think it's wonderful!"

"Wonderful!" repeated Tatler in awed tones. "There's nothing *wonderful* about it! It's downright awful!"

"You try telling *them* that!" muttered Martin, wincing at the sight of a hairy Highlander. "And if you think *this* is awful, just *wait* till you see Edinburgh! I'm telling you, you won't recognize it!"

"It wouldn't be so bad," Tatler muttered in horror, his eyes drinking in the garish dreadfulness of the tartan train, "if all the carriages were painted in the same tartan but ... but they're all different!"

"They're all different inside as well, sir."

"You mean ...?"

"Tartan from end to end," nodded his secretary, "carpets, seats, the lot and," he added, turning pale at the horror of it, "there are bagpipes as well."

"Bagpipes!! They – play – bagpipes – on – the – train?"

"All the way north, I'm afraid, sir." He fished in his pockets and drew out a small envelope. "That's why I brought you these. I thought you might need them."

"What are they?" Tatler regarded him suspiciously.

"Earplugs," said his secretary, hiding a grin. "You're going to need them, believe me. I ... er ... I also bought you these for the journey."

Tatler looked inside the plastic bag. "Sandwiches and bottled water? But surely I can buy these on the train?"

Martin shook his head. "Not any more," he said, his eyes glinting. "They now have what they call a *Scottish menu.*"

"What on earth do you mean, 'a Scottish menu'?"

"Principally haggis, mashed turnips and potatoes followed by shortbread, something called 'Black Bun' and ... and a drink called Irn Bru."

"Iron Brew! What the devil's Iron Brew?"

"I asked that myself when I was in Edinburgh last week and they told me it was made from girders. No, sir," Martin gulped at the expression on Tatler's face. "Seriously! That's what they said!"

By the time the train reached Edinburgh's Waverley Station, Tatler had cause to be grateful to his secretary — for the earplugs, if nothing else! And although he had been forewarned about the changes in Edinburgh, nothing had prepared him for the dreadful reality of a city that positively wallowed in tartan.

"I can't understand why you haven't noticed it, Archie," he said to the Chief Constable the following day. "The castle's the same as before, thank heavens, but the rest of Edinburgh," he flapped his hands helplessly, "seems to be covered in tartan!" He shook his head in disbelief. "Thistles, flags, tartan streamers, banners of all the different clans — they're here, there and everywhere. Bagpipes on every street corner! For goodness sake, Archie, *Hollywood* couldn't do it any better! It's not natural! It's ... it's like *Braveheart* out there! And the people! Kilts all over the place! I ask you!"

Archie Thompson frowned at Tatler across his desk. "We *are* Scottish, you know, George," he said somewhat sharply. "Tartan's very popular. I've even had a request from the Scottish Police Federation to issue tartan trousers to the men. There's a big demand for it! Tartan's fashionable these days!"

"Fashionable!" Tatler looked flabbergasted. "For heaven's sake, wake up, man! It's more than fashionable! It's ... it's weird!"

The Chief Constable, however, not only looked totally unconvinced by Tatler's outburst, he also looked more than slightly offended. So much so that Tatler was visited by a sudden feeling of acute anxiety and thought it politic to change the subject. Mind racing, he sat back in his chair and, taking a deep breath, broached the real reason for his visit to Edinburgh; Duncan Campbell's film of Loch Ness. "Ah well! Down to business!" he said, mustering as much of a smile as he could manage. "You got the film from Campbell, you said?"

"Ah, yes. The film. Yes, Duncan brought it in personally. I hope you don't mind but I've already gone through it with him. He was on his way to film wildlife somewhere in Africa — Kenya, I think, so we went through it before he left. It's quite short, actually. Only lasts a few minutes." He pressed a switch on a TV monitor and they watched as the screen flickered and came to life. As the blue waters of Loch Ness appeared, Tatler leant forward and gave it his full attention.

"Hmm," he said as the Chief Constable rewound it and they went through it again, "there's not much to go on, is there."

"It really only makes sense if Campbell's story about the Loch Ness Monster is true, you know," Thompson said. "Look at this bit, where the water is suddenly all churned up for no apparent reason. He pointed it out in particular. And, as *he* said, the children in that frame," he clicked on "pause" to hold the picture, "are definitely scared. Look at the girl's face!"

"The men aren't too happy, either," Tatler said shrewdly. "Which is the one you recognized?"

"The chap on the right. His name's Sir James Erskine. Totally respectable chap. Has a distillery down by Holyrood Park that makes that fabulous whisky called 'The MacArthur.' You must have tasted it."

Tatler raised his eyebrows and smiled. "I have, indeed," he said feelingly.

"He's an MSP as well, you know. Got elected to the Scottish Parliament last year."

The two men looked at one another speculatively. "He doesn't really seem the type to be mixed up in any funny business, does he," Tatler said. "Still, you never know. Who's the other man?"

"The Park Ranger on Arthur's Seat, a chap called John MacLean. He lives in one of the Park cottages near the distillery so it's perfectly reasonable to assume they know one another. Equally respectable, too, I might add. The children are his, by the way."

"To my mind, it's the children that are the stumbling block," Tatler mused. "Who in their right minds would put their children at risk with dragons around?"

"So you think it could all be perfectly innocent?"

"It could be if it weren't for Duncan Campbell's story." Tatler pursed his lips. "And there *was* a dragon, remember. A plane-load of people saw it."

"Including one of my special constables!" nodded Archie Thompson. He paused, eying Tatler thoughtfully. "I'll get my secretary to make an appointment for us to see Sir James, then, shall I?"

"Yes," agreed Tatler. "Whatever's on the film, I think we have to talk to him anyway."

As the Chief Constable pressed a buzzer to call his secretary, Tatler got to his feet and strolled to a window that overlooked what was now a veritable tartan city. As far as he was concerned, the dragon was now almost of minor importance. More serious by far was the tartan nightmare that seemed to have Scotland in its grip. His secretary hadn't told him the half of it. It was much, much worse than he'd thought. And how on earth, wondered Tatler, could the Chief Constable of Edinburgh, an astute and intelligent man, not realize the freakishness that was being perpetrated under his very nose?

But who or what lay behind this sudden passion for all things Scottish? And it was a passion, of that he had no doubt. A very strong passion. The passengers on the train had convinced him of it. They positively revelled in their tartan clothes, ate haggis with gusto and tapped their feet enthusiastically to the swirl of the bagpipes. It wasn't put on. They were genuine, through and through.

He pursed his lips and frowned; for what really worried him was the fact that he couldn't, for the life of him, understand why!

9. Turkish Delight

"Thank goodness Arthur remembers the way," muttered Hamish, holding a torch aloft as he led a small group of MacArthurs along a narrow, dusty passage, deep under Arthur's Seat. "I haven't been down here in ages."

"Me neither," answered Jaikie, panting slightly. "For goodness sake, give Archie a shout and get him to slow Arthur down a bit. He's galloping along at a rate of knots! I can't keep up and that carrier-thing we've rigged up for the mirrors, is going to start banging off the side of the tunnel if he goes any faster."

Archie, perched on Arthur's back, ducked his head as the light of his torch gleamed on the uneven roof of the tunnel. Hearing Hamish's shout, he twisted round and glanced in concern at the ropes that harnessed a flat, trolley-like affair to Arthur's massive bulk. "Slow down, Arthur," he said worriedly. "You're going too fast! We don't want the ropes to get tangled."

Although Arthur obediently slowed down, the worst was over as the tunnel widened suddenly to reveal a huge, roundish hall. Set into its rocky walls were a series of large, arched doors.

"I remember this cave," Archie said excitedly, slipping off Arthur's back and sticking his blazing torch in one of the wall sconces. The MacArthurs crowded in round the dragon who led them to a door on the far side of the cavern.

Two burly MacArthurs pulled the door open and there was an awed silence as they walked in and looked at the shrouded bulk of the magic mirrors stacked against the walls of the store room.

"Take the covers off and let's see them," instructed Hamish, pulling a length of dusty cloth from one of the mirrors. As the strips of sheeting slid to the ground, the magic mirrors were revealed in all their glory, endlessly reflecting both them and the flames of their burning torches. The mirrors were huge — at least seven feet tall, Jaikie reckoned, gazing up at them in wonder. Their glass had a strange, sparkling sheen to it but the dull, iron frames, decorated with carvings of flowers, birds and animals, were oppressive as well as imposing.

Archie shivered slightly and looked at Jaikie and the others. Although they all knew that the mirrors were locked, they nevertheless had an aura of their own that proclaimed them powerful objects of magic. If one of them were to ripple, Archie thought, no one knew who or what might step through ... or from where ...

Hamish, obviously thinking along the same lines, gestured to the piles of sheeting. "Cover them up again," he instructed shivering slightly, "and let's get them loaded onto Arthur's trolley. And don't, whatever you do, touch any of the carvings or you might switch one on by accident!"

It took at least six MacArthurs to load each one and they were all panting as the last mirror, looped with ropes, was hauled up to the top of the pile.

"Can you pull all this weight, Arthur?" Archie asked anxiously. "They must weigh a ton!"

Arthur looked down his nose at Archie and blew a puff of smoke. "Do me favour, Archie," he said dryly, "I *am* a dragon, remember!"

The pace of the return journey was, nevertheless, a lot slower and, as they followed the trolley, Archie's heart sank as his mind raced over the problems that faced him; for magic mirrors were notoriously tricky things. Each mirror was actually only half a mirror and could only be considered whole when the settings of any two halves matched up. That the other half of the mirror could be on the other side of the world made no difference — if the settings were correct in a few seconds you could quite easily step between towns, cities and countries worldwide. Nevertheless, they had their risks; for if the setting of one half was wrong then you could, as Hamish had said, end up in Outer Mongolia or Darkest Africa, for that matter. And the destructive wave of energy caused by two mirrors locking against one another could cause complete devastation ... Archie shivered at the thought.

"Do you think you'll manage to set them all properly, then?" queried Jaikie, looking at him doubtfully.

"I hope so," muttered Archie.

The Great Hall was a scene of total confusion when they arrived. MacArthurs milled everywhere and had obviously been busy in their absence, for long tables now stretched the length of the hall; gold dishes were being unpacked and polished; delicious smells drifted up from the kitchens and Lady Ellan, looking a trifle frayed as she organized the preparations for the great banquet, waved to them in relief as she saw them start to unload the mirrors.

By the end of the day, the hall was ready. The MacArthur, dressed in robes of fur and velvet, looked round and nodded in approval. Hung with banners and blazing with light from hundreds of torches, the hall was magnificent and certainly befitted the status of their royal visitor. He strode towards the gilded chairs that had been set up in honour of their guest. Arthur, whose scales glowed crimson in the torchlight, moved forward and curled proudly at his side with Archie standing beside him.

The MacArthur then lifted his arms and in a commanding voice, chanted the words of a powerful spell.

Silence fell. By this time, the MacArthurs had all heard that Prince Kalman was in Edinburgh and knew that this could be a dangerous few minutes; for by dropping the protective shield, they were allowing him access to the hill.

Time passed — second by nervous second.

"Are all the mirrors set?" questioned the MacArthur as his crystal ball was placed in front of him.

Archie gulped, nodded and crossed his fingers behind his back as the MacArthur passed his hand over the shining crystal. As it glowed to life, he spoke briefly to Lord Rothlan. "The shield's been lifted, Alasdair. The Sultan can step through now."

Almost immediately, one of the mirrors rippled and a gasp of wonder echoed round the hall as Sulaiman the Red, Sultan of Turkey, stepped through into the great hall, slowly surveying its grandeur before turning to the MacArthur, who, with Arthur accompanying him, stepped forward, bowing low. Lady Ellan curtsied, overawed by the jewelled magnificence of the Sultan's golden clothes. Draped in ropes of pearls, sparkling with diamonds and glowing with rubies and emeralds, he was totally breathtaking. Lifting her eyes to his handsome, bearded face, however, she saw beyond the outward show of his regalia and breathed a silent sigh of relief; for the Sultan's glance, although proud, was both shrewd and intelligent.

By this time, all the mirrors were rippling as, curved scimitars swinging at their sides, the colourful, gaudily-clad figures of the Sultan's Guard jostled and tumbled their way into the hall after their master.

But where was Lord Rothlan, Ellan wondered, her eyes searching the row of mirrors. She saw Sir James step into the hall with an expression of bewilderment on his face that made her smile. Neil and Clara followed with their father behind them, and then Lord Rothlan appeared holding Mrs MacLean by the hand as she stepped through the frame of the mirror into the hall.

Ellan moved forward swiftly and caught her by the hand. "Mrs MacLean," she said warmly, "how lovely to see you, but ..." She looked questioningly at Lord Rothlan, knowing that Mrs MacLean didn't have a firestone.

"Janet got caught up with the Turks in the restaurant," he explained. "She travelled through the mirrors with me."

"We really should have given you a firestone ages ago," Lady Ellan said, apologetically. "We'll all be busy tonight with the Sultan's banquet but I promise you, it's the first thing we'll do tomorrow morning!"

The arrival of the Sultan of Turkey and his court was a glittering event that set the magic carpets in the hill rippling with delight for they had all been made in Turkey in days long past and the power of the Sultan and his crown was woven into their very fabric. His presence renewed their strength and Neil and Clara, thankful to be back in familiar surroundings, could feel the hill sparking with magic as the Sultan walked through its halls.

The feast that evening was an occasion that few would forget. Torches burned brightly in the sconces on the walls, their flickering flames reflected in the glowing gold dishes and bowls that decorated tables now laden with food.

During the course of the evening, Sir James met the MacArthur's eyes and they exchanged smiles of relief at its obvious success. It was, thought Sir James, a scene of almost mediaeval splendour and one that he would always remember.

10. Carpet Capers

It wasn't until after breakfast the following morning, however, that the MacArthur, Lord Rothlan and the Sultan got down to the serious business of the visit. Gathered round an old mahogany table in a panelled room, they started their discussions while everyone else waited, albeit somewhat anxiously, in the Great Hall, wondering what was being said and what plans were being laid.

With a flap of his wings, Amgarad perched happily on Clara's shoulder as she followed Lady Ellan, Neil and her mother to Arthur's cave where the dragon lay lazily on his glittering mound of fabulous treasure. He hissed a gentle welcome to Mrs MacLean as she and Clara scrambled up beside him. Clara urged her mother to rest against one of the dragon's arms while she sat uncomfortably on the treasure itself. Amgarad hopped onto the open lid of a huge box, spilling with golden sovereigns.

"Now we'll choose a firestone for you, Janet," Lady Ellan said, looking round thoughtfully. She rummaged among the treasure and picked out a particularly beautiful firestone from amongst the glowing scatter of emeralds, diamonds and rubies. "I should have given you one earlier but, quite frankly, none of us thought you'd ever need it."

"Thank you, thank you very much!" Mrs MacLean said, holding it up delightedly so that the torchlight made it gleam. "I'll get John to put it on a chain for me like he did with the others. Otherwise, I might lose it." She looked at it wonderingly and again smiled her thanks before placing it carefully in a zippered compartment in her handbag. "Will I ..." she asked shyly, "will I be able to call a magic carpet with it, like the others do?"

"Yes, of course," came the immediate reply. "When we go back to the Great Hall, I'll choose one specially for you."

"That'll be fab!" said Clara. "Then I can see my carpet at the same time."

Arthur scrambled off his pile of treasure to accompany them and by the time they reached the Great Hall, they found several MacArthurs already starting to set the tables for lunch, carrying wicker baskets full of cutlery, plates and glasses. Near the dais, where the MacArthur usually sat, Sir James and the Ranger lounged on cushions, chatting idly to Archie, Hamish and Jaikie.

"What I don't understand," Sir James was saying to Archie as they approached, "was how MacGregor managed to find the Turkish restaurant at all, far less have dinner there."

"I'd say," Jaikie chipped in, "that the Turks were fishing. We put a strong protective shield round Arthur's Seat the moment we found they were in town you see, and when they found they couldn't get near us, *I* think they tried to catch whoever they could."

Archie nodded. "You're probably right," he agreed. "Although he doesn't realize it, MacGregor still has a lot of magic in him. If he hadn't, he'd never have been able to see the sign in the first place, far less get into the restaurant."

"But he couldn't find it afterwards, when he went looking for it," objected the Ranger.

"They probably just made it invisible to him," Archie shrugged. "By then, they'd have realized that he was of no use to them. They couldn't have known, though, that he'd tell *you* about the restaurant." He nodded sagely. "They struck lucky there, actually, for you proved a different kettle of fish entirely. *You*, after all, were wearing firestones! Aye, their gamble paid off in the end," he said smiling wryly.

"We were lucky, too," muttered Sir James, his eyes turning to the tunnel that led to the room where the talks were being held. "If Rothlan hadn't been watching the Turks through his crystal — well, at this moment in time we would probably still be stuck in Turkey with the Sultan."

Lady Ellan's eyes followed his glance as she approached the dais. "Are they still talking?" she queried. "I was hoping some news might have leaked out."

Jaikie shook his head. "Not a thing so far," he answered, "but by my reckoning, they ought to be out pretty soon."

"How on earth do you work that out?" asked Ellan.

Jaikie grinned. "Your father must be onto his third pipe by now and after the fourth, I doubt if there'll be any air left to breathe in there!"

"Let's hope they won't be much longer, then," she said, smiling appreciatively, for her father's addiction to a foul-smelling pipe had long been a source of argument between them. "Actually, we're just going to the back of the hall to choose a carpet for Mrs MacLean. Call me when there's any news, won't you!"

Neil and Clara clapped their hands twice when they reached the side of the cave where hundreds of magic carpets were stacked in neat rolls against the wall. Immediately, two carpets unrolled themselves swiftly and sailed gracefully towards them. Clara patted hers gently and felt the carpet ripple with pleasure. Lady Ellan, too, stroked it fondly. Patterned in an intricate design of red and blue, it had been her carpet as a child and she had chosen it specially for Clara when she had first come into the hill. Now she looked for another and, in the end, selected one with a pattern of birds and flowers for Mrs MacLean.

"There, Janet," she said kindly, "this will be your carpet from now on. Remember, though, you have to be wearing your firestone to call it.

"Can I call it now?"

"Yes, of course," Ellan smiled. "Clap your hands together twice, say 'carpet' and it will come to you."

Mrs MacLean clapped her hands briskly, said "carpet" and watched excitedly as her carpet rose to hover in front of her.

"Why don't you fly round the hall for a while," suggested Lady Ellan. "Until the meeting finishes, we've really nothing else to do."

"Good idea," Neil said delightedly, grinning at Clara as his mother climbed onto her carpet and set off round the vast hall. "It's been ages since we last flew on the carpets! I'd forgotten how totally fab it is. Mind out, Arthur! Here I come!"

Clara nodded in agreement as she scrambled onto hers and prepared to follow her mother round the hall. "I wish we could have another adventure like the last one," she called to Neil. "Life at the moment seems . . . I don't know . . . just plain dull!"

Neil grinned at her and felt the same old feeling of excitement thrill through him as his carpet zoomed through the air. Clara was right. Life *had* been dull of late; nothing but school, school and more school. Now he sat, tense and alert, on the magic carpet and as he whizzed madly round Arthur, he somehow knew that another adventure was on the way.

11. Shocking News

Had Neil been listening to Hamish and Archie's conversation, he would have been even more convinced that another adventure was in the offing, for Archie was telling Sir James and the Ranger of the strange meeting between Prince Kalman and the Frenchman.

"I think your French count must be Louis de Charillon," Sir James said, thoughtfully. "I've met him once or twice, as it happens. In fact, I'll be seeing him in a few days time. The Scottish Parliament is hosting a grouse shoot for diplomats at the weekend and I noticed his name on the list. De Charillon is the French Consul."

"Yes, we gathered that," nodded Hamish. "We followed him back to Randolph Crescent and saw the French flag hanging over his door. The police had to escort him in, you know, for there were crowds of fishermen protesting outside. That Trade Union fellow, Jimmie Leadbetter, was the leader and the language he was using was something terrible."

"I'm not surprised," said Sir James grimly. "Feelings are running high at the moment. But you said you were watching a house ... in Moray Place, did you say?"

"Yes," Hamish smiled, "as pigeons, of course!"

"Actually, I know someone who lives there ... but go on ..."

"We knew it had to be Kalman," Hamish said seriously. "If he hadn't put a protective shield round his house we might never have noticed, but it warned us that something was going on. So we kept watch and that's how we picked up on the French Consul fellow."

"The strangest thing of all," interrupted Archie, "was that when he went into the house, he called Prince Kalman, 'Mr Stuart'."

Sir James choked.

"Are you all right, Sir James?" said Archie, looking concerned.

Sir James choked again, so utterly flabbergasted that he could barely speak. "He called Prince Kalman *what!?*" he spluttered.

"Mr Stuart," repeated Archie.

"You ... you *must* be joking!" Sir James was appalled. "If it's the Stuart I'm thinking of, he couldn't *possibly* be Prince Kalman."

Archie frowned. "It was *definitely* the prince," he said, looking at Sir James strangely. "We felt his magic, you see. It couldn't be anyone else."

"Was he tall, with long, fair hair tied at the back of his neck?"

Hamish nodded. "And he was wearing a brocade waistcoat under his suit."

"That's the man," breathed Sir James. "Good Lord! Ned Stuart! A magician!" He shook his head in wonder. "I really can't believe it!"

"Do you know him then?" asked Archie curiously.

"*Know* him?" Sir James breathed hard. "*Know* him! Of course, I know him! He's an MSP, isn't he? A Member of the Scottish Parliament!" He ran his hands distractedly through his hair. "And you're telling me that he's Prince Kalman! How can he possibly be Prince Kalman?"

Hamish smiled sourly. "Kalman has the crown, Sir James. He can be anyone he pleases." He frowned and drew a deep breath. "The pity is that we have only found out about him now. Do you know how long he has been calling himself Stuart, Sir James?"

"No, no I don't. He's new to the parliament, like me," confessed Sir James, pacing up and down, his mind in complete turmoil. "Very popular he is, too. In fact, he's so well thought of that people are talking of him as a future First Minister! You know, I *really* can't take it all in! Are you *sure* you're not mistaken?"

"Believe me, there's a protective shield round that house that a herd of elephants couldn't shift," Hamish said evenly. "This Ned Stuart fellow *is* Prince Kalman. There's no two ways about it, I'm afraid!"

Sir James turned suddenly and grabbed Hamish by the arm. "The mirrors!" he gasped. "I thought they looked familiar when I saw them in the Turkish restaurant! I remember now! Ned Stuart has at least two in his house. I saw them in his study the last time I was there."

"That proves it, then," nodded Hamish slowly. "If he has such mirrors in his house then there's no doubt that he's Kalman."

"But why would he be entertaining the French Consul?" mused the Ranger. "We're more or less at war with the French these days, aren't we?"

"That's what I thought," agreed Archie

"The prince has a reason for everything he does," observed Hamish seriously. "What *I'd* like to know, is where he's been this past year!"

"Well, if he really is Ned Stuart, then he's been here in Edinburgh," Sir James looked at him in surprise. "I've been to his house several times. He entertains on quite a grand scale."

"Did you ever wear your firestone when you went to see him?" Archie asked, somewhat anxiously.

Sir James shook his head. "No, I usually keep it locked in my desk drawer."

"Thank goodness for that! You might have had a very nasty accident, otherwise!" "You don't think he might have hexed me or something, do you?" Sir James looked more than a little alarmed.

"It's more than likely!" confirmed Archie. "You've had a lucky escape, Sir James!"

"Just as well I didn't wear it then. Really, I only ever use it if I'm coming here and need to call a carpet — or if I think something strange might be happening; like MacGregor's tale of the disappearing Turkish restaurant!"

"Kalman's really being a bit cheeky," muttered Hamish, disgustedly. "Using the power of the crown to hide himself from us is one thing, but to do it here in Edinburgh, right under our very noses ..."

"But why on earth did he put a protective shield round his house all of a sudden?" asked Jaikie, puzzled. "We didn't know he was in town. He didn't need to do it and it was a dead give-away."

"What was a dead give-away?" asked Lady Ellan as she and Clara joined the little group amid a flapping of wings as Amgarad swooped to land on Clara's shoulder.

"Kalman suddenly putting a protective shield round his house."

"The Turks!" Sir James said immediately. "It must have been! Their restaurant was at the bottom of the High Street just yards away from the Scottish Parliament. And it was oozing magic! He must have picked up on it!"

Hamish raised his eyebrows. "I bet that gave him a nasty shock," he grinned. "I know it floored us when we realized that Sulaiman the Red's Turks had set up shop in the High Street! But you're probably right. Kalman would be terrified that they'd latch on to the crown."

"As far as I'm concerned," muttered Sir James, "it

isn't just a matter of us getting the crown back any more. *I* think there's another problem we have to address. If Kalman is involved with the French, then quite frankly I think it's my duty to find out what he's up to. They are pushing their claims to our fishing rights to the brink of all out war, you know. It's no laughing matter."

"You could always merge with the Frenchman and find out what he and Kalman talk about when they're together?" suggested Clara, idly stroking Amgarad's wings.

Archie shook his head. "That wouldn't work, Clara. Kalman would sense at once if anyone had merged with the consul. We'll have to think of something else."

"Surely what we need is someone inside the consulate itself," Lady Ellan mused. "Don't you know anyone who works there, Sir James?"

Sir James shook his head. "Everyone who works there will have been cleared by security. I honestly doubt if we could manage it."

The Ranger, smiling at the sight of the eagle perched on Clara's shoulder, was suddenly visited by a brainwave. "We should send Amgarad! Just look at him, sitting on Clara's shoulder! In an ideal position to read letters and listen to phone calls. Couldn't you magic the count into wanting an eagle as a pet? Or something?"

"Mair like the *or something,*" growled Archie. "And isn't Amgarad a wee bit noticeable? I mean, he's an eagle, for goodness sake."

"Well, he could be a parrot . . or . . . or a canary, I suppose ..." Jaikie looked hopefully at Amgarad who looked so black affronted at the suggestion that the idea was promptly dropped.

"We could mention it to Rothlan," Hamish said

hurriedly, "and maybe, Sir James, you could question the count at this shooting party that you were talking about?"

Sir James nodded. "I only hope he doesn't cry off. De Charillon doesn't have many friends at the moment!"

"Where is this shoot taking place?" asked Archie interestedly.

"At Gleneagles," answered Sir James, naming one of Scotland's most prestigious hotels. "I'm really looking forward to it. I just hope that the rain holds off for long enough to give us a good day. The forecast isn't promising."

12. Magic Words

Lady Ellan turned and smiled a welcome as Lord Rothlan, Sir James and the MacLeans walked into a small cavern that had been hurriedly decorated in the Turkish style in honour of the Sultan's visit. Arthur, curled beside her chair, reared up and hissed softly in pleasure as he saw the children.

"It's just like being in Turkey again, isn't it?" Sir James remarked as they entered; for the walls had been lined with low divans, Turkish carpets lay deep on the floor and several of the ornate brass coffee tables scattered round the room were piled high with large dishes of fruit.

"Bags I sit beside Arthur," Neil said quickly, as he ran to sit beside Lady Ellan. Clara, however, just grinned and moved towards Lord Rothlan so that she could be beside Amgarad.

As the Sultan entered, deep in conversation with the MacArthur, they all stood in respect and, following Lord Rothlan's lead, bowed low.

"The Sultan and I have been discussing the crown," the MacArthur said, settling himself on a divan while Arthur curled himself carefully by his side. "You will all be pleased to hear that Lord Rothlan has agreed to lead a party in a quest to get it back. Ellan will go with him and possibly Jaikie and Hamish." The MacArthur looked doubtfully at Sir James and the Ranger as though hesitant to involve them in danger. "How do you feel about going, James?"

"I'd love to but I really don't see how I can," Sir James said with a frown. "Not only from the work point of view but I think I'd actually be of more use here in Edinburgh. From what Archie tells me, it seems that Prince Kalman is calling himself Edward Stuart. As he's a Member of the Scottish Parliament I want to find out what devilment he's up to. Especially if the French are involved! You know that their trawlers have been fishing illegally in our waters and attacking our boats?"

The MacArthur nodded. "It wouldn't surprise me if Kalman's behind it all — and the very fact that he's had himself made a Member of the Scottish Parliament is a bad sign. Quite frankly," he sighed, "the sooner we get the crown back, the happier I'll be!"

The MacArthur's eyes then turned from Sir James to the Ranger.

John MacLean didn't wait to be asked but nodded immediately. "I'm quite prepared to go, if you think I'd be of any use."

"And us, Dad!" interrupted Neil. "Don't leave us out! We want to go! Don't we, Clara?" said Neil imploringly. "It would be such an adventure and Lord Rothlan and Lady Ellan are going as well!"

There was a hushed silence as everyone looked at the Ranger and his wife. John MacLean heaved a sigh but knew he had to refuse. "I'm really sorry," he said, looking guiltily at the MacArthur, "but it might be quite dangerous."

As the Sultan and the MacArthur exchanged dismayed glances, Sir James spoke hastily. "Maybe we should talk a bit about the risks first," he said. "For instance, where is the crown? Does anyone actually know?"

"If Kalman has magic mirrors in his house then he will probably be keeping the crown at Ardray," Lord Rothlan answered. "He'll have his mirrors set so that he can travel backwards and forwards easily."

"Where *is* Ardray?" Clara asked.

"Ardray? It's in Appin; quite close to Jarishan."

"Is his castle on an island, like yours?" Neil queried.

Rothlan shook his head. "Kalman's castle lies in the middle of a magic forest," he said. "It's actually more of a tower than anything else. The Black Tower of Ardray," he mused. "I used to go there quite often when I was young. Kalman and I were friends in those days. Since then, it seems to have changed a lot. From what I hear, the magic forest is full of goblins now."

"Wow!" Neil's eyes widened at the thought.

"Couldn't you use the mirrors you have here in the hill to get to Kalman's castle, MacArthur?" queried the Ranger.

"That would be risky," was the reply. "Mirrors are not only tricky things to set but they can quite easily be locked against intruders. And if you get caught between mirrors — when both sides are locked, that is — well, that's more or less it! You get held in a kind of limbo land!"

"Won't the crown be protected?" queried Sir James.

The MacArthur nodded. "Its magic will protect it but the Sultan doesn't see that as an obstacle. He knows the magic words that will release it from any spell. Whoever says them will be able to take the crown from Ardray."

"Well, that all *sounds* relatively straightforward," said Sir James, "but how would you get there? On magic carpets?"

"We've talked about that," Rothlan interrupted, "but the MacArthur feels that we would be too easily discovered. Birds and other animals can see magic carpets in the air and Kalman has his spies watching us already. According to Hamish, one of his crows has been patrolling Arthur's Seat, so we have decided that it would be best to travel back in time and only revert to the present when we reach Ardray."

The Ranger looked dismayed. "Travel through time!" he echoed. "But I thought ..." he stammered, "I thought we'd be going by car or by train to the nearest station."

"You'd never get there," Rothlan assured him. "Any train or bus we travelled in would be sure to have an accident and we can't take the risk of innocent people being hurt, you know."

"You'll be well looked after, Ranger, I assure you," the Sultan added. "I'm supplying everything you'll need for the journey — including the finest horses from my stables at Ruksh."

"At Ruksh?" repeated Lord Rothlan and Lady Ellan together, meeting the Sultan's eyes in startled wonder.

Neil met Clara's eyes in rising excitement. No way was he going to miss out on this adventure. A journey through Scotland on horseback! *In the past!*

"It's not actually the journey that worries me, Ranger," the Sultan said dismissively. "It'll only take a few days and you'll travel safely enough with Lord Rothlan looking after you. No, if there is going to be a problem, it'll be with the crown itself; for Prince Casimir, remember, used its own magic against it." He regarded them all seriously. "You see, the fact remains that although it lay for many years in Lord Rothlan's loch, it didn't reveal itself to him, did it? Although it tried to attach itself to Arthur," and here he turned to the dragon and inclined his head, "it didn't stay with him either but, in the end, fell back into the loch and returned to its master, Kalman. The Meridens have a very strong hold on the crown and what I am afraid of is that, after what happened in the loch, nobody here will be able to take it from Kalman, even with the magic words. Except, perhaps ...”

“Who?” asked Sir James, looking at him sharply.

The Sultan looked apologetically at the MacLeans. “The children,” he said.

He raised his hand at the murmur of dissent. “Please let me explain. The children have no magic in their bodies for the crown to react to, but if I implant the words of the spell in them, I will virtually be speaking through them and my words will be powerful enough to break any spell that ties the crown to the prince.”

“Yeeeah!” Neil leapt to his feet, punching the air. “Great! *Now* can we go, Dad?”

Clara, too, looked excited as Neil grabbed her hands and whirled her round and round.

“Clara! Neil! Calm down the pair of you,” Mrs MacLean scolded. “Really, your behaviour! And in front of the Sultan, too!”

Both children collapsed on the divan, their eyes shining with excitement.

“It’s all right, Mrs MacLean,” the Sultan said, his lips curving in a rare smile. “I, too, was young once.”

At this remark, Sir James shot him a speculative glance. Just how long ago, he wondered, had *that* been!

“Perhaps,” suggested Lord Rothlan, “it might be a good idea for Neil and Clara to wait in the Great Hall until we’ve talked this over.”

John MacLean nodded in agreement. “Off you go, you two,” he said. “We’ll call you back when we’ve decided what to do.”

Neil made a face at Clara but they got to their feet willingly enough and walked along the short tunnel that led to the Great Hall.

"What d'you think, Neil?" Clara asked despond-
ently as they plumped themselves down on a couple of
cushions. "Mum'll never let us go. Not in a month of
Sundays, she won't!"

In this, she was mistaken, however, as once Mrs
MacLean heard Lord Rothlan's plan to take the crown
from Ardray, she looked less worried and eyed her husband questioningly.

"Neil and Clara are as dear to us as they are to you,
John," Lady Ellan urged gently. "We'll all protect them
from any harm that might come their way, you know
that. And remember, you'll be with us, after all."

"The Sultan, too, turned towards the MacLeans. "I
know how you both feel," he said, meeting their eyes
understandingly, "but if you allow the children to carry
my words, I assure you that they will be protected
throughout the journey. It's my intention to give each
rider a magic cloak. As long as they are wearing them,
neither heat nor cold, hunger nor thirst will affect
them — and, of course, the cloaks will shield them from
any hexes that may come their way."

"Our plan is relatively simple and straightforward,"
Rothlan said, outlining what they intended to do.
"Kalman may be a powerful magician but even he can't
be in two places at once, you know. The MacArthur will
keep in touch with us through the crystal and when
Kalman's attending an important meeting or a session
in parliament, he'll tell us so that we can go into the
tower and take the crown."

"What about getting through the magic forest,
though? Won't there be a protective shield round it to
keep people out?" the Ranger objected.

"Probably," admitted Rothlan, turning to the Sultan.

"The magic words will destroy any protective shield,"
the Sultan assured him.

"You see, it's really of the utmost importance that we take the crown from Kalman," Rothlan said, his voice serious, "and to be honest, John, I think that giving the magic words to the children is probably our only chance of getting it back at all."

Janet MacLean pursed her lips. She liked and trusted Lord Rothlan and knew that as far as the crown was concerned, he spoke the truth. Looking at her husband, her forehead creased in a worried frown, she said at last. "You'll be with the children, John, and . . . and the Sultan has given us his word."

Although the Ranger looked doubtful, he nevertheless appreciated the truth of what had been said and, seeing the set of serious and concerned faces that confronted him, finally nodded his head in agreement.

The Sultan rose to his feet and shook him by the hand. "Thank you, Mr MacLean," he said gratefully. "I appreciate the trust you have put in us. You will all travel under my protection and need have no fear of the future."

At a nod from the MacArthur, Arthur rose to his feet and made his way to the Great Hall where Neil and Clara sat glumly.

"Up on my back, you two," Arthur said. "I'll take you back to the Sultan."

Neil looked at Clara in dismay as they climbed up onto Arthur's wing and slid their legs over his neck. The dragon's voice gave nothing away and so convinced were they that they wouldn't be allowed to go that they could hardly take it in when their father told them that they, too, would be going on the quest for the crown.

"Gosh, Dad! That's fabulous!" Neil's face shone. "Didn't I tell you, Clara! Didn't I tell you that another adventure was on the way! I knew it! I just knew it!"

The Sultan beckoned Neil and Clara to his side and took their hands in his. The huge ruby in his ring glinted red as his fingers closed over theirs. *"Kutaya Soloi."* The strange words, spoken softly, sent a tingling wave of magic through them and, such was the power of the hex, were no sooner heard than forgotten.

The hawk-like face of the Sultan looked at them gravely. "You now know the magic words that you must say to break the shield round the crown," he said. "I wish you both well."

Neil thought hard and then shook his head doubtfully. "I ... I'm sorry," he said, "I heard you say them but I can't seem to remember them." He flashed an anxious glance at Clara. "Can you, Clara?"

Clara, too, shook her head and looked at the Sultan enquiringly.

The Sultan's eyes twinkled suddenly. "Don't worry," he smiled, "you will know them when you need them, I promise."

13. The Famous Grouse

A few days later, as he watched his secretary, Janice, leave his office at the distillery, Sir James hoped fervently that she hadn't noticed the look of dismay that had crossed his face as she had detailed his meetings for the afternoon. She'd certainly looked suspicious when she'd mentioned that the Chief Constable of Edinburgh, Sir Archibald Thompson, had rung to make an urgent appointment.

Sir James sighed as he leant back in his chair and wondered what on earth he was going to say to Archie Thompson. Just as he had been congratulating himself on the success of the weekend shoot, too. Grimly, he reached for his telephone and dialled the Ranger's number with a hand that shook slightly.

"Come on, answer, blast you," he muttered as the telephone rang and rang.

"MacLean here," the Ranger's voice suddenly boomed confidently down the line.

"John! Thank goodness you're in. Listen, I've just had some bad news and I thought I'd better warn you in case you have a visit from the police."

"The police?" repeated the Ranger, somewhat startled.

"The police," confirmed Sir James. "My secretary has just told me that while I was out, the Chief Constable called to make an appointment to see me this afternoon."

"The Chief Constable!" echoed the Ranger in dismay. "But ... but ... why? You haven't had any more problems at the distillery, have you?"

"Of course not! That was all sorted out last year. Everything's fine!"

"Do you think he's maybe collecting for a police charity, then?"

"For heaven's sake, John, I'm sure he has a lot more on his plate than charity work. What worries me is that there actually could be a very good reason for his coming here and to tell you the truth, I'm sweating at the thought of it!"

"What on earth's that?"

"Remember the night we took Arthur to Loch Ness? When the police stopped the transporter as we were about to leave the park?"

"Don't I just! I thought it was all over for us at the time!"

"Well, I didn't mention it to you then, but the Chief Constable was actually among the police that stopped us. He wasn't in uniform; perhaps he'd been dining nearby and been called out in the general alarm, but I knew him right away. I was at school with a cousin of his and we met up once or twice at cricket matches and the like. I always had it in the back of my mind that he might have recognized me but as nothing was ever said, I thought ... well, I thought I'd got away with it."

"Even if he did see you, James, what can he do? After all, it was ages ago! He can't arrest you for travelling in a transporter with a load of sheep on board. The MacArthur made himself and the dragon invisible. All that the police saw in the back of the transporter were sheep!"

"I know, I know," Sir James muttered, "but pulling the wool over the eyes of the Chief Constable is a serious matter ..."

"James," the Ranger sounded alarmed, "James, you *can't* mention what really went on that night. Heavens man, they'll have you certified! And what can he say, after all? You're a respectable MSP and so are your friends. Chat on about the grouse shooting and the moors and you'll be fine! Anyway, how *did* you enjoy your shoot over the weekend? Did the French Consul turn up?"

"He did, although after reading the headlines in *The Scotsman* that morning I rather think he'd had second thoughts. The press really has it in for him, you know! Lord Rothlan went along to his house just to make sure he didn't change his mind!"

"Rothlan! What on earth did *he* have to do with it?"

"Remember you suggested that we send Amgarad into the French Consulate as a spy?"

"I do. I also remember that Amgarad didn't seem particularly thrilled at the suggestion!"

"Well, Rothlan must have thought it a good idea and talked him into it."

"You're not trying to tell me that de Charillon has adopted a hulking, great eagle as a pet, are you?"

"Not an eagle ... a grouse!"

"You must be joking!"

"I'm not," Sir James grinned, despite himself. "Rothlan cast a spell to *make* the poor fellow join the party so he wasn't in the best of tempers to start with. Not only that, I think Rothlan fixed it so that de Charillon didn't manage to hit a single bird all day. He was completely devastated as he's generally reckoned a pretty good shot and although I kept telling him it wasn't the end of the world, he knew quite well that everyone was laughing at him behind his back."

"Stands to reason, doesn't it," commented the Ranger.

"Ah! But he got his grouse in the end! And he didn't shoot it! That's what finished everyone off."

"What on earth happened?"

"Well, visibility was starting to get bad and, when the last flight of grouse flew over, De Charillon missed again. Then there was another burst of fire and when I looked up I saw a last, solitary grouse weaving its way towards the butts in a hail of gunshot. Well, I just knew it was Amgarad, didn't I."

"Amgarad? A grouse?"

"Believe me, you never saw a plumper, fatter grouse than this one! How it managed to get off the ground, I'll never know. Everyone at the butts was trying to blast it out of the sky and, of course, nothing was hitting it. It actually," and here Sir James choked with laughter, "... it actually circled round once or twice and then side-slipped down onto de Charillon's shoulder — and stayed there!"

"And then what happened?"

"Well, dear Louis looked so absolutely thunderstruck at getting a grouse at last that everyone on the shoot just rolled around laughing. It was all Rothlan's doing, of course, and Amgarad had a whale of a time acting the part later on in the evening. Talk about the Famous Grouse! You've never seen anything so funny in your life!"

"So diplomatic relations have been restored then, have they?"

"How right you are! De Charillon was the hero of the hour and as far as I know, Amgarad is now positively lording it at the French Consulate and the chef has been given strict instructions not to put him in the pot.

14. An Official Enquiry

Sir James was still smiling at the memory of de Charillon's astounded face when Janice showed the Chief Constable and another soberly-suited gentleman into the office.

Relieved at her employer's relaxed and cheerful demeanour, she left the men together with a light heart and went to prepare their coffee. She wouldn't have been quite so happy, however, had she popped her head round the door half an hour later, for by then the Chief Constable had asked some very pertinent questions and Sir James was beginning to stammer.

"The thing is, James, that on this film that we have, you're seen talking to someone. Someone who ... er ... isn't there."

"I must have been talking to the Ranger."

"No, the Ranger is behind you at the time."

"I must have been talking to myself then," Sir James said unhappily.

"We also have an eye witness who saw the Loch Ness Monster by the shore and," the Chief Constable continued bravely, "what looked like a dragon."

"Aren't we entering into the realms of fantasy here?" Sir James did his best to look surprised.

George Tatler held up his hand and spoke for the first time. "Sir James, enough of all this evasion." He leant forward in his chair and looked Sir James straight in the eye. "The sighting of a dragon and the Loch Ness Monster is peculiar enough but it's my belief that there's a lot more to it than that! Something very strange is going on in Scotland just now and quite frankly it has me seriously worried. I usually know what's going on, and where and why, but this time I can't, for the life of me, put my finger on anything."

Ignoring the Chief Constable's outraged expression, he continued. "Archie, here, doesn't seem to think anything out of the ordinary is happening, but I ask you, Sir James, haven't you *looked* at Edinburgh lately? I mean, *really* looked at it? Haven't you seen the tartan everywhere?" he gestured vaguely. "Pipers playing the bagpipes on every street corner. People knocking back shortbread by the ton and Irn Bru by the gallon. Men wearing the kilt and tartan taxis plying the streets! It's like a Hollywood version of *Braveheart* out there and there's no sensible reason for it!

Sir James pursed his lips. "It's the City Council you want to be talking to," he said, clutching desperately at straws. "It's probably just a gimmick to attract the tourists."

Archie Thompson nodded in agreement but Tatler was so incensed that he almost jumped out of his chair. "It – is – not – a – gimmick!" he found himself shouting. "It is not a gimmick," he said in a quieter tone, sinking back into his chair. "Look, I've been among them and what I found is that the people buying haggis *want* to eat it. The people buying tartan carpets for their houses *want* to buy them. It's as though someone has cast a magic spell over the whole country ... and it's dangerous."

Sir James found himself sweating slightly at the reference to magic spells but Tatler's words nevertheless gave him pause for thought. As his heart sank suddenly and his face whitened with shock, he looked at the man in utter horror. Come to think of it he *had* thought the sudden passion for tartan that seemed to have gripped the country, rather strange. But was Tatler right about it being a spell, he wondered? Could Kalman really be behind it all? With his mind in absolute turmoil, Sir James automatically repeated Tatler's last word.

"Dangerous," he said, dazedly, raising his eyebrows while striving to get a grip of his thoughts. "Surely it isn't dangerous. If people want tartan carpets in their houses, I don't see the harm in it."

"Do you have tartan carpets in your house, Sir James?" interrupted Tatler.

"Well, no," Sir James admitted.

"Have you eaten haggis lately?" he continued.

"No, no I haven't."

Tatler looked at him through steely, grey eyes. "In a recent poll, a staggering one hundred per cent of Scots said they had eaten haggis at least once in the past week! So how are you different from the rest of your countrymen, Sir James?"

"I didn't read that anywhere!"

"It was a secret poll and, let me tell you, it has the Prime Minister worried! And believe you me, she has quite enough on her plate at the moment, what with the French fishermen doing their best to start an out and out war in the North Sea."

Sir James shrugged. "That's politics," he said.

"Look, Sir James," Tatler pleaded anxiously, "please come clean with us. You were in that transporter and you're our only lead in this business. We *know* there was a dragon; it so happens that one of Archie's special constables was on the BA flight that night and saw it quite clearly. Now from our point of view, it isn't so much the dragon that's of interest, it's the fact that it didn't show up on radar *and* it didn't show up on the Loch Ness film. Anything that doesn't show up on radar and disappears on film, interests us. Do I make myself clear?"

"But *I* don't know why it didn't show up on your radar," Sir James said helplessly. And then realized what he'd said.

The Chief Constable leant back in his seat and almost grinned. "You were never a good liar, James!" he smiled. "Come on now, out with the whole story!"

Sir James, cursing his stupidity, looked at them worriedly. "It's not my story to tell," he said slowly, "and, quite frankly," he added with feeling, "it isn't at all what you're expecting to hear either, believe me."

"We thought that maybe someone had invented a new chemical solution that counteracts radar," encouraged Tatler, gesturing vaguely. "Was it something like that?"

Sir James shook his head.

"Perhaps you could tell us where the dragon-like creature came from then?" ventured the Chief Constable. "We're well aware that people smuggle exotic animals into Britain from time to time, and if you're frank with us we probably won't press charges. In fact, I can assure you that we won't!"

"Well?" queried Tatler gently.

Sir James looked at the two men ruefully and wondered what on earth he was going to say. The fact that both he and the Ranger had been caught on film was a serious business and although their questions had been friendly enough so far, there was a grim purposefulness about the two men that boded ill if he continued to prevaricate. But, on the other hand, if Ned Stuart *had* cast a spell over Scotland, to say nothing of being up to some sort of skullduggery with the French, the two men might well, in the end, prove useful allies. And surely, if he did arrange for them to meet the MacArthur, they would hardly be likely to talk about it afterwards. A belief in faeries was, after all, one of the quicker ways of losing one's job ...

"It's nothing like that at all," he said, breaking the silence, "and if ... if I do tell you what actually happened, I want your word of honour that you won't pass it on; either of you!"

Both men glanced at one another swiftly and nodded in agreement. Tatler eyed him speculatively and with growing interest; he sensed that something he'd said had hit Sir James hard but what it was, he couldn't quite gauge. The man, however, was obviously shaken and he had no doubt at all that what they would now hear from him would be the truth.

Five minutes later, however, he was not so sure.

"*Faeries?*" Archie Thompson almost spat the word out. "Under *Arthur's Seat!* Do you *really* expect me to believe a tale like *that?*"

"Not really, no," Sir James almost grinned at the flabbergasted expression that adorned the Chief Constable's face. Used to hearing many a strange tale, this had nevertheless taken the feet from under him. As the Chief Constable struggled to reconcile the notion of faeries, dragons and magicians lurking in what, to all intents and purposes, was his backyard, Tatler's agile brain was working swiftly; for Sir James's information, mind-boggling as it was, did much to make sense of an otherwise unbelievable scenario.

Avoiding the eyes of the Chief Constable, he took a deep breath. "Prove it, Sir James," he said quietly.

Meeting Tatler's shrewd, grey eyes, Sir James came to a swift decision and opening a shallow drawer in his desk, drew out his firestone. Pushing back his chair, he got to his feet and, watched closely by the two men, walked over to the tall windows that looked over Holyrood Park and the immense bulk of Arthur's Seat.

Fervently hoping that he was doing the right thing, he opened one of the windows wide, clapped his hands twice and said "carpet."

"And just what was that meant to do?" the Chief Constable asked suspiciously as he returned to his desk.

A curious smile twisted Sir James's lips as he regarded them both speculatively, wondering just how they were going to react when a magic carpet sailed in through the window. "Just wait a few moments and you'll see," he grinned, perching casually on the edge of his desk.

Tatler and Archie Thompson exchanged glances and both were visited by the uneasy and, it must be said, totally unfamiliar feeling, that somehow they had ceased to dominate the interview. Tatler sat, tense and alert, ready for anything but even he was taken completely by surprise as the magic carpet brushed its way through the window and gently swooped to hover beside Sir James.

The two men leapt to their feet in amazement and stared round-eyed as the carpet rippled and swayed about three feet from the floor.

"Welcome to the world of magic, gentlemen." Sir James savoured the moment. It wasn't often, he thought, that one was given the opportunity of reducing high-ranking officialdom to a state of gibbering idiocy. Indeed, both men seemed to be unable to talk coherently and Sir James's lips twitched as the Chief Constable stretched out his hand to touch the carpet with an expression on his face that strongly suggested that it might bite.

"The thing is," Sir James said, looking at the carpet doubtfully, "I don't know if this carpet can carry all three of us and I also feel that I should ask the MacArthur's permission before I take you into the hill.

Can I ... would it be all right if I were to leave you for, say, ten minutes?"

"Of course, Sir James," the Chief Constable actually managed a weak smile as he looked at the carpet with fascinated eyes. "You've given us enough to talk about for a couple of hours, far less ten minutes!"

Sir James sat down on the carpet and, by so doing, he and the carpet immediately disappeared. As Tatler and the Chief Constable started in amazement, Sir James quickly got off again. "I'm really sorry," he said, "I should have told you that I'd become invisible when I sat on the carpet. It's quite normal, I assure you."

"Normal!" Tatler's voice echoed his disbelief. "Nothing about this is at all normal!"

It was almost half an hour, however, before Sir James returned with two other carpets rolled up in front of him, for initially the MacArthur hadn't been at all keen at his bringing officialdom into the hill and had said so in no uncertain terms.

"These people have to make reports, Sir James," he said sternly, "and before you can say Jack Robinson, the whole world will know about us and Arthur. I can just see it! The hill will be mobbed by people trying to get in to see what we look like."

"You said you knew this man when you were at school," interrupted Lord Rothlan. "Can we trust him, do you think? Would he keep our secret?"

"As Chief Constable, Alasdair, he's a man who knows hundreds of secrets," Sir James answered, "and as a person, I would trust him. I'd never have suggested bringing him here otherwise."

"And the other fellow, the Englishman ... George Tatler?"

"I should imagine that he knows even more secrets than Archie Thompson," Sir James said dryly. "By the way," he broached the subject nervously, "he seems to think that someone has cast a spell over the whole country to make Scotland more Scottish than usual!"

There was a pause as Rothlan and the MacArthur looked at one another speculatively.

"Actually, I did think it all a bit strange," Rothlan admitted, "but I didn't see the harm in it. It didn't enter my head that it might be a spell."

"Well, if it wasn't either of us, it must have been the prince," the MacArthur frowned grimly at the thought. "And he must have had a good reason. It's only the magic of the crown that could keep a spell like that in place for any length of time."

"I can't understand why," Rothlan murmured, frowning slightly. "Maybe it might be a good idea to meet these friends of yours, Sir James. If you're sure they'll keep quiet about us."

"They will, I'm sure," Sir James assured him, "after all, rambling on about faeries in Arthur's Seat is hardly in their interests, given the positions they hold."

"Aye," agreed the MacArthur, "there's always that!" He pondered the matter for a few moments and then shrugged resignedly. "Well, when all's said and done, Sir James, we can't have you being arrested by the Chief Constable now, can we? Especially after all you've done for us! Here, Jaikie," he called, beckoning him over, "bring me a couple of firestones and two more carpets for Sir James, so that he can bring his friends into the hill."

15. Bonnie Prince Charlie

Louis de Charillon's office had, until that moment, been a scene of complete tranquility. The great seal of France adorned the wall behind his desk; tall windows with looped and tasselled curtains looked over a street, empty of protestors; flower arrangements perfumed the air and the ornate, gilt furniture reflected the elegance of a bygone era.

The silence was such that Amgarad, firmly ensconced on the count's shoulder, found his eyes closing and, shifting on his claws, made a clicking noise with his beak. The count's hand came up to ruffle his feathers and Amgarad nibbled his ear gently in return. In the few days he'd been in the consulate, the count had managed to earn his profound respect and, indeed, it was well merited as de Charillon was meticulous in his scrutiny of the most boring legal documents, was a demanding but fair master and never lost his temper.

The buzz of the fax interrupted the silence and, noting the crest on the top of the paper as it came through the machine, the count rose with a sigh to read the latest edict from Paris.

Amgarad read it with him and such were its contents that he almost toppled off de Charillon's shoulder. The count's reaction was much the same. He scanned the paper, disbelief written large across his face.

"Incredible!" he muttered, tossing it none too gently on his desk and moving again towards the fax that was spewing out yet another sheet of paper. "Totally incredible!" He shook his head. "Ned Stuart! A prince!! I was so *sure* his documents were forgeries!"

Amgarad, who had fluttered onto the desk, eyed the sheet and began clicking and snickering softly to himself as he read the document aloud, secure in the knowledge that someone in the hill would be watching him through the crystal.

When Hamish heard what Amgarad was reading he gave a shout that brought Lord Rothlan and Lady Ellan running towards him. Arthur, too, raised his great head and ambled towards the crystal to see what all the fuss was about.

"Is Amgarad all right?" queried Rothlan, as he peered into the crystal.

"He's fine, but for goodness sake let me get what he said, down on paper."

Seeing the little group clustered round the crystal, Jaikie ran up. "What on earth's happening?" he demanded.

"It's unbelievable!" Rothlan snapped as he listened to Amgarad's words. "The French authorities have just authenticated Ned Stuart's claim to be the direct heir of Charles Edward Stuart and a Prince of the Blood, no less!"

"Bonnie Prince Charlie!" gasped Jaikie. "He's aiming a bit high, isn't he?"

"Look!" Hamish muttered, grasping Lord Rothlan's sleeve. "Look! Amgarad's lifting the other sheet. It's got a drawing on it!"

"It's the crown, the Sultan's crown! It must be! Look at the rubies on it!"

Such was the concentration of the little group clustered round the crystal that they failed to notice the arrival of Sir James, Tatler and the Chief Constable as they sailed into the hall on their magic carpets.

Sir James eyed Tatler and Archie Thompson as they swooped into the ornate splendour of the vast cavern.

He was glad that their first sight of it was so impressive for the hall, still hung with all the banners and trappings of the Sultan's visit, looked totally magical. They feasted their eyes on the incredible scene but although the crystal ball glowed brightly on its stand by the dais, surrounded by a milling crowd of MacArthurs, it was not this that fascinated them. What held them totally riveted was the sight of Arthur in all his glory. Tatler turned chalk white and the Chief Constable swallowed hard as they both stared thunderstruck at the sight of the wonderful dragon whose presence dominated the hall.

Sir James hid a smile as they scrambled off their carpets. "Come over and meet Arthur," he invited. "Don't worry, he won't harm you."

Arthur hissed a welcome and blew a puff of smoke down his nose as Sir James approached and bowed to him. The Chief Constable and Tatler followed suit and eyed him warily as they were introduced. "Is this ...? Is this ... *the* dragon?" whispered Tatler, "the one from Loch Ness?"

Sir James nodded as he looked round searchingly for the MacArthur. "Yes," he said, "this is Arthur. He lives here in the hill."

As the MacArthur was nowhere in sight and everyone's attention seemed to be fixed on the crystal, Sir James shepherded them through the crowd to where Lord Rothlan and Lady Ellan stood transfixed at the scene unfolding in its glowing depths. Tatler and Sir Archie exchanged glances as they eyed the little people covertly and looked at Sir James with new respect. He certainly hadn't been exaggerating when he'd told them of the magic inside Arthur's Seat.

"What's Amgarad saying now?" Hamish whispered in frustration. "Quiet, everyone, I can hardly make him out."

They watched with fascination as the count retrieved the drawing of the crown from Amgarad's beak and looked at it frowningly. The little grouse then perched on his sleeve and snickered busily away as he read the writing underneath.

Hamish translated Amgarad's chatter. "The crown has been identified by an Islamic scholar as being identical to an old sketch in the archives of the Topkapi Museum in Istanbul. It is not Scottish, as Stuart claims, but is an old Turkish crown dating from the seventh century. We would be interested to know how Stuart came to have it in his possession."

"So that's what he's up to," Rothlan breathed. He hit his palm with his fist and looked at Ellan in dismay. "Why didn't I think of it before? The arrogance of the man! He wants to be King of Scotland!"

Sir James cleared his throat. "I rather think these gentlemen might be interested in helping us, Lord Rothlan. May I present the Chief Constable of Edinburgh, Sir Archibald Thompson and Mr George Tatler."

Rothlan, assessing the two men at a glance, bowed abruptly. "I'm sorry," he apologized, shaking them both by the hand. "You must have heard what was just said and, quite frankly, I'm still in shock! But I'm very pleased indeed to meet you. Our host, the MacArthur, is busy at the moment but this is his daughter, the Lady Ellan; and Jaikie and Hamish, his lieutenants."

Lady Ellan curtseyed formally and shook their hands. "My father won't be long," she promised, "but perhaps I can offer you some refreshment?"

The Chief Constable bowed and it was only with difficulty that he kept his glance from straying towards the crystal. "No, thank you. I've just had coffee with Sir James." He turned to Lord Rothlan, "I ... er, don't wish to pry but did I hear you say something about a King of Scotland?"

Rothlan nodded and looked enquiringly at Sir James. "How much do Mr Tatler and the Chief Constable know?"

Sir James shook his head. "Not a lot," he admitted.

"Then why don't you show them the crystal and fill them in while I go and find the MacArthur. The Sultan's just brought the horses of Ruksh through the mirrors and plans to return to Turkey once Archie's got them stabled. Ellan and I must be there to say goodbye to him, you understand. Gentlemen, forgive me, but James will tell you the whole story."

As he and Ellan left the hall, Sir James turned to Jaikie and Hamish. "Don't go away, you two. I'm sure the Chief Constable and Mr Tatler would like to get to know you better and have you translate Amgarad's cheeping for us. The hill seems to have been busy while I was away. I haven't a clue what's been happening."

Tatler, totally fascinated by the glowing crystal, threw Sir James a glance that mixed wonder with naked envy. "I don't suppose they have any of these for sale, do they?" he asked wryly. "The Foreign Office, I know, would give an arm and a leg for one!"

"An arm and leg," expostulated the Chief Constable as they bent over the crystal. "Heavens above, man, they'd give half the Defence Budget!"

"Just a second!" interrupted Tatler, "isn't that what's-his-name?"

Archie Thompson peered closer, "De Charillon, yes ... and *that's* the French Consulate! How very interesting! I've wanted to know what's been going on in there for weeks now," he muttered, watching de Charillon pore over his faxes while Amgarad swayed gently on his shoulder.

"That's never a grouse, is it?" Tatler sounded amazed.

Jaikie couldn't resist it. "Actually," he said with a sidelong glance at Tatler, "it's an eagle."

Sir James choked back his laughter. "It's all right," he said taking a quick look at George Tatler's affronted face. "He's not being rude. I know it sounds incredible but, actually, it *is* an eagle." He sighed deeply. "And with that, I've just realized what an awful lot of explaining I have to do if I'm going to fill you in on all this before Lord Rothlan comes back. Why don't you leave the crystal just now? Hamish will call us if anything happens."

"Who exactly is this Lord Rothlan?" queried Tatler.

"He's one of the faery Lords of the North and according to the MacArthur, the best magician he's ever met."

Tatler and the Chief Constable eyed Sir James uncertainly but as he gradually explained everything that had happened in the past, their faces reflected a wonder and incredulity that was followed by a grudging acceptance of what they were hearing ... and, in the end, acute concern.

"... and the crux of the matter as far as I'm concerned, is Ned Stuart and what he's up to with the French," finished Sir James.

"You mentioned that he's been meeting with de Charillon, but has he actually been *conniving* with the French?" the Chief Constable sounded doubtful.

"You'll remember that I mentioned a Prince Kalman? Well," Sir James looked at them shrewdly, "we just discovered a couple of days ago that he's Ned Stuart! They're one and the same person."

"Ned Stuart! A magician? I don't believe it!" The Chief Constable threw the idea out of the window immediately.

Sir James shrugged. "But you didn't believe in all of this, either, a couple of hours ago, did you?" he said, gesturing round the vastness of the great cavern.

The Chief Constable swallowed. "No, no, I didn't," he agreed. "And I must admit that it's only since I've been here that I've come to realize how strange this tartan business actually is. I can't believe that half an hour ago I thought it all quite normal!"

"That's because you've got a firestone in your pocket," Sir James explained. "Even I was affected at first and didn't think the craze for tartan was all that odd, but then I don't usually wear my firestone. It was only when I put it on to call my magic carpet that the enormity of it really hit me. It must be Kalman's doing. He's a wily character and, believe me, it's a cleverer spell than you think!"

"You mean that this Prince Kalman — I mean, Ned Stuart — cast a spell?"

"Yes, I do. And the strange thing about it is that it only seems to affect the Scots," Sir James pointed out. "George wasn't affected by it because he's English."

"Good Lord!" Tatler breathed.

"And it was something that *you* said, George, that put me on to it," Sir James explained. "You talked of Scotland being under a Scottish spell and although I'd thought it strange that everyone should go haywire all of a sudden over tartan and haggis and the like, it didn't, as I said, enter my head that it was deliberate. But now, I've come to the conclusion that it *was* deliberate, and there *is* a reason behind this sudden passion for all things Scottish. A very good reason!" he gestured towards the crystal. "I knew it the minute I heard Amgarad read the papers that came through on the fax. They confirmed that Ned Stuart is a direct heir of Bonnie Prince Charlie and a Prince of the Blood. He isn't, of course, but given the atmosphere he has created in Scotland just now, there isn't a Scot in the country who won't support him. The people will accept him as their king with open arms, believe me!"

"But they can't do that!"

"I wouldn't bank on it."

"People power can do anything these days, George," muttered the Chief Constable. "Sir James is right. We're in deep trouble!"

16. Kitor Listens In

The following morning, Sir James slammed his copy of *The Scotsman* down on the breakfast table with such force that half of his morning cup of tea slopped into the saucer. The newspapers were full of the story! His horrified eyes scanned screaming headlines and, leafing through the pile, he found that photographs of Ned Stuart decorated the front pages of every one of them. It was the columns of the *Times,* however, that he found the most worrying as it led with the announcement that once the College of Heralds upheld his claim, Stuart would ask the Scottish Parliament to endorse his right to the throne of Scotland!

Sir James muttered under his breath, looked at his tea in disgust and rose from the table. "Sorry about the mess, Mrs McGuire," he said weakly as the housekeeper came in to clear the table. She looked at him sideways, well aware that his bed hadn't been slept in that night, and wasn't at all surprised to see him stifling a yawn as he prepared to attend his first meeting of the day. Stuffing a pile of papers into his briefcase, he nevertheless knew that he wouldn't really need them as the problems of Edinburgh's crumbling sewers paled before the latest and most exciting topic of conversation. Ned Stuart, King of Scots! Parliament would be buzzing with it!

Sir James breathed deeply and stared unseeingly round the room. It couldn't be allowed to happen! Knowing Kalman's power, however, his heart sank and, indeed, the only thing that gave him any comfort at all was the knowledge that Rothlan and his little band had left the hill at dawn that morning for Ardray.

Sir James shivered as he thought of it. He'd spent the night inside the hill, chatting to the MacLeans, whilst Jaikie and Hamish made the necessary preparations for the coming journey and the MacArthur and Lord Rothlan pored over the formula of the magic spell that would take the little band into the seventeenth century. "It'll only bind us for a short time," the MacArthur explained to Sir James, "then the hill and Edinburgh will return to normal. But the riders will remain in the past until Rothlan casts a spell to bring them back into the twenty-first century again."

Neil and Clara were so excited that they could hardly sleep, but by the time morning came and they were awake and dressed, the MacArthur had already cast the spell that had turned the clock back.

Sir James had found it an unsettling experience. Accustomed as he was to living in a large, thriving, prosperous city, it was a throat-catching experience to stand on the slopes of Arthur's Seat and look through the thin, grey light of dawn at the pathetically small stretch of buildings that clung round the castle rock and hugged the ridge that tapered downhill towards the imposing palace and abbey at Holyrood below. Although it was early, wreaths of smoke drifted from a few chimneys and, below the castle rock, he glimpsed the old Nor Loch glinting in the first glimmer of light, with rough woodland stretching from its shores towards the distant, grey gleam of the Firth of Forth.

When Rothlan and his party finally appeared on horseback from the mouth of the tunnel, there was a great cheer from the MacArthurs who had gathered on the hillside to see them leave. Tossing their proud heads nervously, the jet-black horses came to a stamping halt on the slopes of the hill and their grandeur made Sir James wish that he had, after all, agreed to go to Ardray.

Feeling the breeze on his face, Rothlan pushed back the hood of his cloak and, resting a gloved hand on one of the strangely-curved pommels that rose horn-like from the front of the saddle, moved over to Sir James. "Keep an eye on Amgarad for me, won't you?" he said, leaning over the horse's neck. "The only thing that lets me leave him with an easy conscience is the fact that you know de Charillon! I've told Archie to keep you up-to-date with what's going on at the consulate."

"I wish I were coming with you," Sir James said enviously. "But don't worry about Amgarad. I'll not neglect him."

"Goodbye, Sir James," Lady Ellan moved her horse forward.

"Goodbye and good luck, Lady Ellan." He turned to say goodbye to the Ranger and the rest of the group and, noticing that Mrs MacLean was looking upset now that the actual parting had come, put an arm round her comfortingly. "The children will be fine, Janet," he said soothingly. "Everyone will look after them, don't worry."

"I know," she said, a sob catching in her throat.

"Bye, Mum!" Neil called, pulling on the reins so that Chakra, his horse, reared and pranced. "We'll be back soon!"

"You won't be going at all if I see you behaving like that again, Neil," his father said, reprovingly. "Now calm down and act responsibly, for goodness sake!"

Neil looked shamefaced. "Sorry, Dad," he said. "It's just all so . . . unreal, somehow."

Clara, her eyes shining with excitement, bent her head and kissed and hugged her mother. "Isn't my horse wonderful?" she said, stroking the horse's silken coat. "Her name's Sephia. Isn't that lovely? Lady Ellan's is called Rihan, but Lord Rothlan's," she said, turning to look at the great black stallion that carried Lord Rothlan, "Lord Rothlan's is called Rasta."

"You will take care, won't you, Clara?" her mother spoke hastily. "Promise me!"

Clara made a face. *"Of course, I will, Mum,"* she muttered. "I wish you wouldn't keep fussing all the time! Look," her face cleared suddenly, "we're off now! Goodbye, Mum," she urged her horse forward. "Goodbye, Sir James. Take care!"

The MacArthur gave the signal for departure and quietly waved and nodded goodbye to Neil, Clara and their father as they followed Lord Rothlan and Lady Ellan. Jaikie and Hamish brought up the rear and everyone was suddenly silent as the black horses of Ruksh picked their way down the steep hillside. All the riders were dressed in long, hooded cloaks made of a strange, greyish material that gave them a sinister, fearful appearance. Indeed, Rothlan had told Sir James earlier that the Sultan's magic cloaks would not only protect them from hexes but, among other things, would also keep out rain and the most vicious cold. More importantly, by changing colour according to the background scenery, the cloaks would render them virtually invisible as they travelled.

Suddenly feeling guilty that she had been so snappy with her mother, Clara twisted hurriedly in the saddle as they moved down the hill and waved at her frantically. "I'm sorry, Mum," she called. "Take care and don't worry! We'll be back soon with the crown!"

Kitor, a black crow roosting on a nearby crag, had woken up only a few minutes previously, roused from sleep by the sudden noise from the side of the hill. With a fast beating heart, he hopped cautiously closer to see what was going on and not only saw Clara as she turned in the saddle, but also heard what she said quite clearly. Such was his surprise that he almost fell over. There was no mistake about it! She had mentioned the crown! Although horrified at her words, relief flooded through him. After weeks of patrolling the hill with nothing to show for it, he at last had some information to give Prince Kalman.

Peering anxiously over the edge of a nearby rock, Kitor was just in time to see the backs of the seven hooded horsemen as they disappeared downhill. His eyes glistened as he watched them go but many minutes were to pass before he dared make a move, and it was only when the MacArthurs had straggled back into the hill that he felt safe enough to launch himself over the green slopes of Arthur's Seat, towards his master's house.

Shaken to the core at having almost slept through such an important event, Kitor hadn't actually realized that he had been affected by the MacArthur's time-spell and gave such a squawk of horror when he noticed that the Edinburgh skyline had fundamentally changed that he almost fell out of the sky. He fluttered round in dismay as he looked at the new, totally unfamiliar scenery. Not only had the bulk of Edinburgh completely vanished, but what was left of it seemed to lack what, to him, was an essential commodity. Surely, at this time of the morning, cars should have been out, crowding the roads and providing him with breakfast? His black eyes bulged with dismay. What on earth was going on? All of a sudden there seemed to be no roads; just dirt tracks and horses!

It didn't take Kitor more than a few minutes to work out that he had somehow landed in a completely different century and that his life of ease and comfort was over. No roads! No motor cars! *No breakfast!* The enormity of the situation took even less time to register, for Kitor was a bright bird, and with fast food in the shape of squashed rabbit and hedgehog already looming in his bird brain as delicacies of the past, he almost cried at the unfairness of it all. In fact, it was so long since he'd had to kill anything for food that he felt ever so slightly squeamish. A rabbit, perhaps? A small rabbit that wouldn't put up too much of a fight?

He landed on a buttress of rock that overlooked a grassy hollow where he knew rabbits sometimes played and thought vengefully of the MacArthurs. "The MacArthurs," he muttered angrily. "They did this with their spells and their magic! I'll ... whoops!"

The hill beneath him gave a sudden shudder and seemed to fragment before his eyes as the MacArthur's spell wore out and brought Edinburgh back to the present. The grass rippled and then settled once more to stillness. Two baby rabbits popped out of their burrow and looked around in puzzled wonder but despite his hunger, Kitor ignored them for, as he looked towards the city, he not only saw that Edinburgh had returned intact but also heard that most wonderful of sounds — the roar of the morning traffic.

Relief pulsed through him as he soared into the air and headed for the New Town and Prince Kalman; for, hungry though he was, the affairs of the prince came before the pleasures of searching the park roads for his breakfast.

17. Ambush

When they reached the level ground at the foot of Arthur's Seat, Rothlan bore towards the north-west and for a while they cantered swiftly along dirt tracks that bordered cultivated strips of ground. Neil and Clara were glad of the high pommels on their strangely-curved saddles and held on to them tightly until they became more used to the even motion of the horses.

Clusters of poor dwellings clung to the skirts of the city but, as the horses effortlessly ate up the miles, the hamlets gradually became fewer and more widely spread. It was only when they had reached the safety of thick woodland that Rothlan slowed the pace. Clara wrapped the long cloak more firmly round her as they cantered on, for winter was setting in and the weather was chill.

Although the horses did not seem to tire both Neil and Clara soon found themselves losing interest in their surroundings as one stretch of woodland followed another. They did stop from time to time as they made their way steadily northwards, but always in a desolate part of the countryside and usually beside a stream so that the horses could drink.

Neil started to feel hungry and, knowing the contents of the saddlebags that hung over each horse, longed for lunch! Rothlan must have read his thoughts for he pulled up as they reached the top of a steep hill and looked down on an open stretch of country.

"Not far to go now," he said cheerfully. "We'll stop

and have lunch by that river down there, can you see it?"

Looking down, Neil could see the glint of water and breathed a sigh of relief. It wasn't far.

"I don't know about Neil and Clara but I'm starving," laughed Lady Ellan. "All this exercise has given me an appetite!"

They followed a winding path down the steep hill but it was a good half-hour before the stream was reached.

"Here we are," Rothlan said, tugging gently on the reins as they rode into a clearing, beside a gently flowing river. As Hamish and Jaikie dismounted, looping the reins over the saddles so that the horses could graze, Lady Ellan looked round appreciatively. The Ranger, too, nodded as he scanned the leafy glade in front of them. It was a pretty place with an even, grassy bank sloping towards the water.

Clara's legs buckled under her as she dismounted and she grabbed at the saddle for support. "Don't worry," her father smiled, "your muscles will toughen up as we go along. Come and have something to eat."

They ate hungrily as the fresh air had given them an appetite but there was plenty of food and it wasn't long before they felt full. "I'll keep what's left for a snack later on," Ellan said as Clara looked round, wondering what to do with the rubbish.

Rothlan read her thoughts. "Pack it up and we'll take it with us, Clara. It wouldn't do to leave anything lying around that could betray us. You never know, we might be followed."

"Followed?" the Ranger looked startled. "You don't think anyone will find us here, do you? It's so isolated."

"We all use birds as messengers," Rothlan answered. "Who's to know if one of them is not quite what it seems."

"Have you been this way before?" asked Neil. "I mean, did you know this ford was here?" he gestured at the rippling water.

"I've travelled this road many times," Rothlan admitted, "which is why I found it so easy to bring you here by tracks that are rarely used."

Clara shivered. "It's all right being with you," she said, "but I'd hate to travel round on my own. It's so lonely, isn't it?"

Lady Ellan frowned slightly as they made ready to leave. "This isn't the twenty-first century, Clara," she said, swinging herself into the saddle, "it's the seventeenth, remember? Everyone here travels in groups. Robbers, I'm afraid, are a fact of life."

"Especially in the Highlands," added Rothlan. "The hills are full of secret roads. Stealing sheep and cattle from neighbouring clans is almost a way of life."

Ellan smiled. "That's different though. It's a hobby as much as anything else," she observed indulgently.

Rothlan nodded in agreement, scanning the path ahead as he urged Rasta forward.

Although neither Neil nor Clara were aware of it, he had been careful to keep a constant look-out as they made their way north and didn't dare relax his vigilance; for although they had so far travelled unmolested, he knew that they hadn't necessarily passed unseen. In this, he was right, for although few in number, the sight of the strangely-cloaked riders on their jet-black horses had given many a robber pause for thought. Not only did the horses themselves look as though they'd come straight out of the king's own stables but there was something about the riders that made the bravest man shiver.

Darkness was starting to fall when Rothlan swerved onto a track that was better used than most. They were among the hills now, in sheep country, and since lunchtime the horses had been climbing steadily. He knew that Neil and Clara were tiring by the way they slumped in the saddle. The track not only bypassed a small village but was also a more direct route to the shepherds' hut that he had ear-marked as their refuge for the night.

"Keep going," he encouraged. "We haven't far to go now."

Thank goodness, thought Clara wearily. She was tired and longed to stretch out and sleep. So far the only event of any consequence had been the sight of a couple of rotting sheep carcasses. The smell had almost turned her stomach and Neil had covered his nose with his cloak, muttering about the awful pong!

Had they passed along the winding track a little later, they might well have missed the ambush. Indeed, the robbers that lay in wait for unwary travellers had been on the point of giving up their vigil when the tightly-knit band of riders appeared. As it was, the rough-looking bunch of men sitting astride small, but sturdy, ponies looked up with interest on hearing the thud of hooves. Neither was their leader, a gaunt, thin man with a shock of unkempt red hair, intimidated by their sinister appearance. He swung his mount round and watched as the band of cloaked horsemen made steady speed towards them. "Fine horses mean rich pickings," he growled. "Let's go!"

With a great yell and a thunder of hooves, he and his men charged down the hill. Hearing the thud of hooves,

Lord Rothlan looked up. "Robbers!" he shouted, warn-ingly, "ride on, all of you!" He pulled his horse to one side and, as they passed, the sudden flash of a hex crackled in the gathering gloom.

The robbers' ambush was well planned for even as the horses lengthened their stride, hidden members of the band emerged from behind bushes at the side of the track and flung themselves at the horses' bri-dles.

Clara screamed, terrified, as a long-haired, bearded ruffian appeared at her side, hands outstretched. At any moment, she expected to feel his hands grasp her arms and pull her out of the saddle but, to her astonishment, nothing happened. The fellow, his face a sudden mask of fear and disbelief, was still there but somehow he just couldn't reach her. It was as though a sheet of glass lay between them — except, of course, that there wasn't — and although his legs were pounding the ground beside her she realized that he didn't seem to be making any headway at all. Sephia, was steadily moving away from him — as were Neil and the others.

Shaking with fright, she glanced upwards and saw that much the same thing seemed to be happening to the horsemen careering down the slope. With all the shouting and screaming that was going on, it took their leader some time to work out that although they were all galloping hell-for-leather down the hillside, they weren't actually getting anywhere fast. His heart pounded in unaccustomed fear. In fact, they weren't getting anywhere at all! The ground seemed to be mov-ing under the horses' hooves, right enough — he could see it with his own eyes — but the track at the bottom of the hill was as far away as it had been when they'd started.

Pulling his horse up with a jerk, he watched in disbelief as the black horses pulled away unharmed and disappeared at a gallop round a bend in the track.

The rest of the band pulled on their ponies' reins and gathered fearfully round their leader. "What happened, Colin?" one of the robbers panted, panic-stricken, as they crowded round.

"How did they stop us from getting down the hill?" demanded another, his voice scared and fearful.

"Their leader must have been a magician ..."

The ruffian, who had tried to pull Clara off her horse, panted up. "No, no, they were *witches*," he gasped. "There was a girl on that horse! She was a witch for sure! I couldn't touch her, however hard I tried!"

"They looked more like ghosts than witches, " shivered another. "Grey ghosts on black horses."

"Satan's spawn," hissed Colin fearfully. "And what are they doing here, that's what I'd like to know!"

"It wouldn't surprise me if it was the devil himself," another cried forcefully, his face as white as a sheet. "Demons, that's what they were!"

"Rubbish, Angus," their leader growled angrily. "Did you no' see the flash of light? Yon was no' the devil! They were magicians, I tell you, that's what they were!"

"You mean ..."

"I mean," snarled Colin, "that we was hexed!"

Some looked convinced and nodded agreement but the ripple of disbelief that ran through the rest of the crowd was palpable.

Angus looked stubborn. "They were devils, I tell ye," he shouted, looking round as though he expected Old Nick himself to be standing behind him. "Devils!" he repeated, his face contorted with fear. "I don't know about the rest of you," he said, glancing at the circle of petrified faces, "but I'm getting out of here. This place is accursed!"

And, as the men shifted uneasily in their saddles and looked fearfully down the track, the word "devil" hung dark and unspoken in the threatening shades of the night.

18. As the Crow Flies

Kitor flew over woods and fields, grumbling away to himself. In fact, to say he was not at all amused is putting it mildly. If he'd had an ounce of common sense, he told himself disgustedly, he'd have kept his mouth shut and told the prince nothing of the MacArthur's time spell. As it was, the prince had listened to him with sharpened interest, passed a hand over him to gauge the length of the time-spell the MacArthur had cast and promptly sent him back to track down the seven mysterious horsemen!

So, here he was, in the flipping seventeenth century again, with an empty belly and not a road in sight! The knowledge that he only had himself to blame for his predicament merely served to make his temper worse until he reminded himself that his fate could have been yet more terrible. After all, Kalman could have killed him. It was his own fault, he knew, for feeling guilty at having falling asleep while on duty, he had been tempted to embroider his story until, under the increasingly ironic gaze of the prince, his voice had finally stuttered and stammered to silence. Even now, he trembled at the memory as he had fully expected Kalman to blast him to smithereens there and then. He had seen the prince idly point a finger at other birds that had displeased him and to this day, their dying squawks of agony were imprinted on his brain. Especially, he thought, tears dimming his eyes, those of Cassia, a pretty crow that he had had an affection for. Resolutely, he thrust her from his memory and flew anxiously on. If he failed in this mission he might yet meet the same fate and fear surged through him at the thought.

Grimly he continued his journey, his eyes raking the landscape for the band of grey-clad horsemen that he had seen leaving the hill.

Nevertheless, he mused, it was a strange affair, for had he not known the strength of his master's powers, he could have sworn that, when told of the mysterious riders, a shade of unease, even fear, had briefly flitted across the prince's arrogant features.

"Find the riders, Kitor," he had been told. "I will keep in touch with you through the crystal!" And now, here he was, looking for a band of horsemen that could be anywhere. Indeed, the only thing he knew for certain was that they would be travelling north-west; for the prince had obviously guessed their errand and had told him that they would be making for his home at Ardray, amid the mountains and glens of Appin.

Kitor flew until tiredness and the gathering gloom forced him to rest for the night. The sleep, however, did him good and although he woke next morning feeling refreshed, he was also more than slightly peckish. Soaring into the air, he continued his journey and when a cloud of black shapes circling a distant hillside attracted his attention, it was the thought of a free meal more than anything else that made him decide to investigate further. Feathering his wings, he slanted through the air towards the whirling birds and by so doing, found his first clue.

The crows were feeding on the remains of a couple of sheep, eating until they could hold no more; for winter was fast approaching and they knew its hunger. Ignoring Kitor as he swooped down to join the feast, he fed with them until a disturbance in the road raised them all in a flapping, squawking cloud into the branches of a nearby tree.

Annoyed at having his meal disturbed, he looked down at the slow-moving convoy of horses, carts and people passing below. "What's all that about?" he asked idly, puzzled at the sight of the rickety carts, piled high with an assortment of belongings. "Where on earth are they going at this time of year?"

One of the crows, whose grossly distended stomach had made take-off a nightmare and flight almost impossible, gave a long and truly dreadful belch. "Don't know," it said unhelpfully, "but, you're right, it *is* the wrong time of the year for them to be travelling. Winter's on the way!"

"Good riddance to bad rubbish," another said, eyeing the rag-tag band of ruffians. "They're robbers, that's what they are."

"*I* know why they're going," a crow perched on a nearby branch, chipped in loudly "They're scared! Dead scared! I heard them talking when they were packing up their camp." Heads turned as the crow preened his feathers tantalizingly.

"Go on, then," croaked another. "Don't keep us hanging on!"

The crow glanced round and, observing his interested audience with satisfaction, decided to play to the gallery. Always inclined to the dramatic, his eyes glistened as he adopted his best raven-of-doom attitude and said in a hoarse, blood-curdling whisper. "Some of them said that the devil himself rode by last night and cursed them. That's why they're leaving."

"The devil?" There was an anxious flapping of black wings among the branches.

"Something *did* happen last night," agreed one of the other crows more prosaically, "but I don't think it was the devil. There was a flashing crack of light and some horsemen passed through. It was almost dark, so it was difficult to see anything."

"I saw them," interrupted another crow, staggering along a branch that bent perilously under the weight of its belly. "Their leader was a magician! Must have been," he hiccupped, "for he hexed that lot good and proper."

"Were they ..." Kitor couldn't believe his luck, "were they riding black horses?" he queried hopefully.

It nodded. "Black as the night!"

Kitor thanked the crow, relief shining in his eyes at such good fortune. He couldn't believe that he'd found them already. Filled with excitement, he flapped heavily into the air and proceeded to follow the crow's instructions. Finding the track proved easy enough and it wasn't long before he was winging his way along the route that the mysterious horsemen had taken.

Flying on such a full stomach proved heavy going and although he almost wished that he hadn't eaten quite so much, he consoled himself with the thought that he had no idea when or where he would find his next meal. More important was the news of the riders! His spirits brightened considerably at the thought that he had managed to find their trail. He relaxed insensibly; instead of dreading Kalman's interrogation, he now looked forward to it! The prince would be pleased with him and might even reward him.

19. Flying Horses

Clara stared at the towering peaks in awe for the heather-covered heights that now surrounded them were very different from the soft, rolling hills of the south. The horses of Ruksh grazed by the edge of a loch while they ate and it was only when lunch was finished that Rothlan took out a crystal, no bigger than a tennis ball, from one of the saddlebags. Holding it carefully, he passed a hand over it and as it pulsed with light, Archie's face appeared.

Lady Ellan watched Rothlan's face grow taut as he listened to the news from the hill and she felt fear grip her. What could have happened? She moved over to stand beside him but by then the crystal had already misted over.

"What's happened?" she asked fearfully, laying a hand on his arm.

He covered it with his own and met her eyes gently as she blushed and tried to draw it away. "There is nothing wrong in the hill," he said, "all is well there, I assure you, but Archie has been keeping watch over us and he says that we are being followed by a crow; one of Kalman's spies. He thinks it's probably Kitor."

"Is ... is he sure it's following us?"

"Quite sure."

"What are we going to do?" She found that her hand was still in his.

He smiled down at her. "We must change our route," he said gently. "I had hoped that we might have an easy run through the valleys but it looks as though we'll have to take to the mountains after all. Take heart, my dear. If we cross this loch tonight," he comforted her, "we might, with any luck, manage to throw our feathered friend right off the scent! Come, let's tell the others."

The Ranger looked at him, his face puzzled, as he broke the news. "But how can we cross the loch?" he frowned. "We've no boat and it must be miles wide ... and what about the horses? I mean ..."

"Relax," he smiled. "The horses will take us across the water."

"You mean they're going to swim across?" asked Neil.

"No," Rothlan's eyes danced, sensing the excitement that his announcement was going to incur, "we are going to fly across!"

"Fly!" Neil and Clara looked at Rothlan in astonishment and rising excitement.

"Now you know why Ellan and I were so surprised when the Sultan told us that he was giving us horses from Ruksh," he smiled. "It was an unheard of offer. I doubt if he has ever lent these horses to anyone — ever."

As they all turned their heads to look at the elegant animals that grazed contentedly by the water's edge, Clara stated the obvious. "They haven't got any wings," she observed. "How on earth are they going to fly?"

"They can grow their wings whenever they wish," Rothlan assured her, "but in the meantime I think we should press on. The loch narrows considerably to the north and there are fewer islands."

"We're going to fly over in the dark?" the Ranger questioned.

Rothlan nodded. "We mustn't be seen or the crow will follow us. I want him to waste his time trying to find us on this road."

They pressed hurriedly on through a forest track that hugged the shores of the loch, the trees shielding them from view. Clara drew her cloak around her as the weather changed and the wind rose in tearing gusts, pushing banks of dark, angry clouds over the mountains.

As darkness fell, they halted by the sandy shores of a tiny bay. In the fitful light of the moon, they could see that it curved gently round to end in a high bluff of rock that offered some shelter from the wind.

"Shall we have a quick bite to eat before we fly over the loch?" Lady Ellan suggested as they dismounted.

Rothlan nodded. "Good idea. The horses, too, Hamish; they'll need the extra energy if they're going to use their wings."

The Ranger opened one of the heavy saddlebags and Lady Ellan hurriedly handed round packets of sandwiches that they ate standing up, their backs to the wind. Neil's eyes gleamed with excitement as he watched Hamish and Jaikie slip nosebags over the horses' heads and heard them snuffle contentedly as they munched at their oats.

"How do they grow their wings?" he asked, almost bouncing up and down with excitement.

Hamish grinned. "You'll see in a minute, Neil. Don't be so impatient!"

Rothlan strode up, his cloak billowing in a sudden gust of wind. He patted Rasta's neck and paused. "All ready to watch the big event?" he smiled.

Neil nodded, hurriedly gulping down the last of the sandwich, but it was only when the horses had finished eating and everything was safely stowed in the saddle bags that Rothlan lined the horses up, facing the waters of the loch.

"*Serai,*" he said briefly.

The horses pawed the ground and then, from their shoulders, great wings spread and grew until they almost dwarfed the horses themselves. As Rasta's wings flapped huge and black in the darkness, everyone moved, absolutely fascinated, towards the winged beasts.

"Sephia," whispered Clara, her eyes shining, "how beautiful you are! And your wings ..."

Sephia flapped her wings slowly. "Don't worry, Clara," the horse assured her in a whinny of sound, "they are strong and will carry you safely."

And Clara, who hadn't quite known what to expect, felt relieved as she saw that the horses' wings weren't anything like the light, delicate affairs she associated with birds. Indeed, there was nothing fragile about them. They were sinewy and strong, and it was only their feathers that were soft and pliable to the touch.

"*Selis,*" Rothlan said calmly. And they stood back as the horses' wings seemed to fold into themselves and disappear.

"That," said the Ranger, shaking his head in wonder, "is the most fantastic thing I've ever seen."

"Now you must try it for yourselves," Rothlan instructed. "Say the magic word and your horse will grow its wings for you."

They all turned their heads and eyed one another in excitement. "*Serai,*" they said together and, as the black horses of Ruksh grew their mighty wings once more, a shaft of moonlight swept briefly through the clouds, shining silver on the pale sand, the winged horses and the fluttering cloaks of the hooded riders.

The magical scene, however, was not to last. Banks of black clouds, rolling across the sky from the west, soon obscured the moon and minutes later, a squall of driving rain swept dismally over the waters of the loch.

"Pity it's raining," the Ranger murmured, drawing his cloak around him and glancing up at the sky.

"That won't worry the horses," Rothlan smiled. "The blessing is that the heavy clouds will hide the moon and we are more likely to be able to cross unseen."

Rothlan made them wait until it was really dark before they mounted their horses and, as she slipped into the saddle, Clara understood the reason for their strangely curved shape and the need for the two pommels that curved upwards on either side of the horses' necks. She grasped them gratefully to steady herself as, one by one, the horses galloped over the sandy foreshore and, wings flapping majestically, took off into the blackness of the night.

"What do you mean, you've lost them?" snarled the prince.

Kitor turned as white as a black crow can turn. "Milord, truly, they have disappeared. I've searched the roads many, many times from Loch Lomond to the north and there's no sign of them anywhere!"

He waited, trembling in the light of the crystal, for the thunderbolt that he was sure was coming his way.

"Have you asked the crows in the area to keep watch?"

"Master, it was the first thing I did!"

Prince Kalman's brain worked swiftly. Although he had guessed from the start that Rothlan must be one of the riders, he hadn't mentioned the possibility to Kitor, seeing no point in putting him into a panic. He looked at the trembling crow and thought irritably that he would have to be reassuring or Kitor would be of no use to him at all. He was the only one to have seen the riders and he couldn't afford to lose him.

"Just how noticeable are they, Kitor?" he said, making his voice pleasant and reasonable. "Maybe the other crows have let them pass without telling you? There must be many such groups of riders crossing the Highlands, after all."

"Master, they are very noticeable. Not in themselves, for they wear cloaks that hide them but they cannot hide the horses. They are the finest horses I have ever seen; great, black animals that never seem to tire."

There was a silence that lasted so long that Kitor actually thought he was done for. He trembled violently and shut his eyes so he would not see the blow coming. Then his master's voice came from what seemed a very long distance away; a strangely strangled sound.

"Kitor," it was little more than a whisper, "Kitor, it is not your fault that you lost them. Leave the valleys. They must suspect that they are being followed and will have taken to the mountains." There was a pause as the prince thought further. "To get to Appin, they'll have to pass through the lands of the Campbells," he said, eventually. "Why don't you wait for them at Inveraray, Kitor? I'll keep in touch with you through the crystal."

Kitor swallowed convulsively at the reprieve and tried his best to look capable and intelligent for, although he could only hear his master's voice, he knew from the light that held him in its glow that the prince was still watching him through the crystal. His claws gripped the branch he was sitting on so hard that he was afraid it might break under the pressure, and it was only when his master bade him farewell and the glow faded that he relaxed his grip and sobbed with relief.

In Edinburgh, Ned Stuart put the crystal ball to one side and for many minutes gazed blankly into space.

Black horses. Fine black horses that did not tire! A tight ball of fear gathered in his stomach. Could they be the flying horses of Ruksh?

He rose and strode agitatedly round the room. Fool that he was to have thought that the Turks had disappeared with their restaurant! Yet it made no sense that such horses could have come from Arthur's Seat — for the Turks, after all, were just as much the MacArthur's enemies as they were his. And hadn't the MacArthur put a strong protective shield round the hill the minute he'd discovered they were in town, just as he himself had done round his own house?

But the horses of Ruksh!

How it had happened, he'd no idea but there was no getting away from it. The Turkish Sultan and the MacArthur must have joined forces against him. How else could Rothlan and his men be riding the horses of Ruksh?

He threw himself down in an armchair and crossed one immaculately-clad leg over the other, his face a cold mask. All was not lost. He still had the crown and his plans were almost complete. Nevertheless, he shifted unhappily at the thought that he was going to have to hurry things along. Much better to let the proof of his birth filter out bit by bit. There was nothing, he knew, that anyone could dispute — not the age of the paper he'd used, nor the ink; and he'd even been careful when travelling back in time, to write all the documents in the exact year of his supposed birth.

But how long, he wondered, would the Heralds take? Events were moving much faster than he had expected and, just as he couldn't afford weeks of deliberation over his claim, neither could he afford to let Rothlan get within striking distance of the crown. He frowned. There might be a way, though! His friend, Cri'achan

Mor, lived on the road to Appin and was surely powerful enough to deal with Alasdair Rothlan.

He stroked his chin thoughtfully. If he made those
doddering old fools in the College of Heralds verify his
claim immediately, then he could easily do the rest. At
least, he smiled somewhat ruefully, the Scottish spell
seemed to be working well; too well, perhaps, for it certainly hadn't been his intention to reduce Edinburgh to
some sort of Scottish theme park. He shrugged. As long
as it served his purpose, that was the main thing — for,
with the spell in place, he knew beyond any shadow of
doubt, that the people of Scotland would uphold his
claim to the throne and support him to a man! And
as he'd long ago made plans to keep the English seriously preoccupied, his imminent rise to power seemed
to have a good chance of success, despite Rothlan's
untimely interference!

He rose abruptly and, throwing out his arms dramatically, drew on the power of the crown to cast a couple
of very powerful spells.

20. A Cunning Plan

Rising from his desk in alarm, Sir James strode to the window as a pigeon beat a frantic tattoo on the glass with its beak. Pulling it wide, he shivered as a blast of cold air penetrated the room and hastily closed it again as the pigeon flew in.

"What on earth's the matter?" he asked abruptly as Archie materialized before him.

"We've got problems with the French!" Archie said hurriedly. "Amgarad's just given us some really mind-boggling news from the consulate. The MacArthur thinks you should get in touch with the Chief Constable and his friend and use your carpets to come into the hill. Right now!"

"Right now?" queried Sir James. "The Chief Constable and Tatler have a lot on their plates at the moment. You *do* know that the College of Heralds have upheld Stuart's claim to the throne of Scotland?"

"We heard!" Archie grinned. "Believe me, the MacArthur almost blew a gasket! But you must come right now, Sir James. It's really important! Even yon French fellow is almost having a nervous breakdown!"

"De Charillon? Why?"

"A fleet of French trawlers is heading for the North Sea and, from what Amgarad says, the bulk of the French Navy is escorting them."

Sir James looked appalled. "I rather think I feel like de Charillon," he said, sitting down suddenly and reaching weakly for the telephone.

Half an hour later, they were all in the hill gazing through the crystal at a distraught de Charillon who was pacing his office, cursing furiously. Amgarad eyed him apprehensively from his desk as he blasted several high-ranking French ministers to hell and back, including his boss!

"War!" he said to Amgarad furiously, thumping his desk so hard that the little bird bounced. "There will be war! That imbecile Bruiton! He's not fit to run a kindergarten, far less a country!"

The Chief Constable and Tatler looked at one another grimly, their faces strained and white. "Radar will have picked up the fleet by now," Tatler said. "I only hope the navy is prepared for this! It's unbelievable! The French must be totally out of their minds!"

"Don't blame the French, Mr Tatler," the MacArthur said abruptly as Arthur arranged his huge bulk beside his great chair. "This has nothing to do with the French. This is the prince's doing, I'm absolutely sure of it!" He sighed and shook his head. "He must have Bruiton under a pretty strong spell, that's all I can say!"

"A spell?" Tatler looked at him sharply.

The MacArthur nodded. "Think about it!" he said. "The prince isn't a fool. By causing an international incident on such a grand scale, he'll divert attention away from his claim to the throne, won't he?"

"You could be right, at that," Sir James answered.

A note of horror coloured Tatler's voice as realization dawned. "And by the time the government sorts out the French, he'll have had himself crowned King of Scotland!"

"Aye, he's obviously got it planned down to the last detail," the MacArthur nodded. "But don't worry. I'm not going to let him get away with it." He looked at Tatler and smiled grimly. "You tell the navy to stay at home, Mr Tatler, and I'll do the needful. It won't take *me* long to sort out the French."

George Tatler glanced at the Chief Constable and looked at the MacArthur in dismay. "But MacArthur," he protested, "that's impossible! In the first place, it's not my business to give orders to the Admiralty and in the second ... well, no one would believe me! How can I say that ... that faeries are going to protect us from the French fleet?"

The MacArthur, however, was adamant. "You tell yon wuman that runs the country," he said forcefully, "that we are on her side and she's not to do anything. Tell her to keep the British fleet in port and do and say nothing. She must behave as though everything is normal."

"Normal!" Tatler's voice rose shakily. "Normal! With French trawlers and the French Navy in our territorial waters? They've been playing merry hell with our boats for months now and yet you want us to do and say *nothing*?"

"She won't buy it," the Chief Constable agreed. "Not the kind of lady to sit back and do nothing with a French fleet on her doorstep."

"What do you plan to do, MacArthur?" invited Sir James. "Maybe if you were to tell us what you have in mind, it might make a difference."

The MacArthur gave a smile of incredible cunning. "Aye," he said, "sit down and listen and I'll tell you what I was thinking."

And he told them.

The three men looked in blank amazement at the MacArthur when he'd finished outlining his plan. "Well," he demanded, "what do you think?"

All eyes promptly turned to the great dragon who, to give him his due, looked completely and utterly flabbergasted at his unexpected role in the MacArthur's cunning plan. Archie looked at the MacArthur and then at

Arthur, his face a mixture of complete dismay coupled with rising hilarity.

"Arthur could do *that*?" Sir James queried in amazement.

"Well, yes . . . with Archie's help, that is."

Archie threw up his hands, half-horrified and half-laughing at what he was being let in for. "MacArthur," he said helplessly, "you do my head in, sometimes. You really do!"

Tatler, his brain working with lightning swiftness as the beauty of the scheme dawned on him, gave a slow, almost reverent smile.

"Good Lord!" he said in wonder, "I've never heard anything like it! But I know this," he turned to the Chief Constable with hope rising in his heart, "it'll do for the French! It'll do for them completely!! They'll go out of their minds!"

"And," added Sir James pointedly, "if *we* keep mum, they'll never be able to say a word without admitting that *they* started it all!"

Tatler's eyes gleamed with unholy joy at the thought of putting a few French noses out of joint. "I told you! I told you!" he thumped his knee to emphasize his words. "It'll finish them off! By heavens, the PM will buy it! She won't be able to resist it! It's a master stroke!"

They looked at one another in rising excitement. It *was* a master stroke.

The thought of the entire French government seething in a fury of total frustration and unable to vent its rage was suddenly too much for Tatler. He gave a strange neighing sound and a snort of pure, undisguised glee that promptly set the others off. "Can you imagine ... aaaah, haaaa?" he choked, wiping the tears from his eyes. "Ahaaa ..." he gave another strange whinny and rocked back and forwards, shaking convulsively and flapping his hand as he tried to speak and couldn't. Sir James, too, creased up and laughed until he cried, clinging helplessly to the Chief Constable who, doubled up with mirth, was mopping tears from his eyes.

The MacArthur didn't know whether or not to look offended at this rather doubtful reception to his cunning plan and seeing the expression on his face, Sir James managed to gasp out reassurances. "MacArthur," he said, wiping the tears from his eyes, "MacArthur, we think it's a *wonderful* plan."

Once the laughter had died down, however, Tatler became serious. "Are you quite sure you can manage it?" he queried. "I ... er ... I happen to know Charles Wyndham, the head of MI5, quite well. A nice chap; very efficient. But I've got to be sure you can manage it, if I'm going to persuade him to put your plan to the Prime Minister."

21. Hell's Glen

Rothlan pulled up his horse as they reached the head of a bleak valley.

"Are we near Inveraray yet?" the Ranger queried as they gathered behind him.

"Not far now," Rothlan assured him. "We'll save a lot of time if we take a short-cut through this glen."

Clara swallowed as she saw the sheer drop that lay before them. She felt suddenly sick with fear and gripped the pommel tightly. On their journey across from Loch Lomond she hadn't been able to see much in the dark and had trusted to the horses, but now that they were travelling in daylight, the whole majesty of the mountains lay before them and their heights were awesome to say the least.

Rothlan pointed to the grey glint of the sea that glimmered in the distance. "By my reckoning," he said, "that should be Loch Fyne. It's a sea loch and Inveraray Castle lies on its furthest shore. This," he gestured to the lonely, strangely sinister valley that swept bleakly below them, "this, I think, is called Hell's Glen by the locals. We needn't be afraid of anyone spotting us here," he said grimly. "It's uninhabited. The name speaks for itself!"

He looked over at Neil and Clara, guessing their unspoken fear at the dreadful drop that lay in front of them. "If I go first and you see how the horses cope, will it be easier for you?" he asked, for there wasn't all that much room for take-off. If the worst came to the worst, the horses might literally have to step into a void and fall until their wings held them and they flew.

Neil shot a sidelong glance at Clara and nodded. He felt just as scared as she did.

"*Serai!*" Rothlan said sharply. They watched in wonder as, in a matter of seconds, Rasta's wings sprouted, grew and unfolded. The black horse, edging itself back as far as it could against the side of the mountain, flapped its great wings strongly and then, galloping forward, soared into the air over the breathtaking drop. Rothlan flew round towards them. "You'll be fine," he called, "the horses know what they're doing!"

The Ranger went next and Neil and Clara relaxed as the great horse leapt effortlessly into the void, its wings beating strongly. "You'll be all right," he called as the winged horse circled in front of them. "Don't look down, Clara! Shut your eyes and hold on!"

"*Serai!*" Clara said fearfully, gripping the pommels on either side of the saddle and shutting her eyes tightly. She felt the brushing movement of Sephia's wings as they unfolded, the swish of air as the horse beat them strongly and the thud of its hooves on the rough turf. Then the noise ceased and she knew that they were flying.

One by one, the horses of Ruksh grew their wings and flew from the top of the mountain, circling slowly downwards into the valley below. Clara only opened her eyes when she felt Sephia's hooves hit the ground and sat shaking in the saddle as she looked up and saw the great height from whence they had come. "*Selis,*" she instructed, so that the horse's wings folded and disappeared.

"Okay?" Neil queried, urging his horse towards her at a trot. Then he, too, turned and followed her glance upwards. "That was really quite something, wasn't it?"

Now that they were down in the valley itself, they dismounted; glancing round uneasily, for the place had an eerie feel to it. The silence was absolute. No birds circled the lofty peaks and even the stream seemed to run silently down the length of the valley.

Jaikie walked the horses to the water and watched in alarm as they tossed their heads and snorted, backing away from the stream. "Milord," he called anxiously, "the horses will not drink!"

Rothlan walked over and looked frowningly at the horses that were shying nervously away from the fast-flowing water that ran black and deep over the rocks. He met Jaikie's eyes and they both knew that something was desperately wrong, for the horses would not refuse to drink for no reason. His face became suddenly serious as he scanned the valley and the grim sides of the mountains that suddenly seemed to lower threateningly over them.

"I've heard tell of this glen," he muttered, "but I never really believed what was said about it."

"What was that?" Lady Ellan asked.

"People say that it's the home of the Man of the Mountains, and that he values his privacy!"

"The Old Man of the Mountains?" queried Neil as they looked round apprehensively — and to all of them it seemed as though the mountains loomed closer than before.

"According to legend, he is King of the Cri'achan," Rothlan said grimly. "They were stone giants that used to walk the hills in ancient times. Locals call him the Old Man of the Mountains and no one lives here for fear of him."

"It's certainly a grim place," the Ranger said, looking round at the oppressive peaks that surrounded them.

Lady Ellan gave a shiver of fear as a sudden malevolence seemed to thread the atmosphere.

Rothlan felt it, too. "We won't stop to eat," he said, his eyes scanning the heights. "I don't like this glen and neither do the horses. Let's mount and go."

Hamish and Jaikie looked at one another and agreed. Living as they did in the depths of Arthur's Seat, their feeling for the earth was strong and they sensed an evil presence among the towering peaks.

"You're right, milord," Hamish said, with fear in his eyes. "We've got to get out of this glen quickly. Something is stirring in the mountains; I can sense it."

"Wrap your cloaks around you and let them cover as much of the horses as you can," Rothlan snapped as a strange wind soughed through the glen. "Come on, let's go!"

The black horses of Ruksh stamped and tossed their heads as they, too, sensed the change in the atmosphere. As Rothlan urged them forward, they immediately rose to the gallop, their hooves pounding the rough grass and heather as they headed for the distant glimmer of the sea.

Clara and Neil clung grimly to the pommels on their saddles as the horses streaked alongside the banks of the rushing, black stream that tore hungrily between deep banks. With devilish intent, it kept changing its course in front of them so that horses had to take great leaps to clear it. Rushing winds suddenly screamed from the heavens, tearing at their cloaks, but more frightening still was the growing rumble of sound that seemed to come from the very depths of the earth. It grew in volume, reverberating between the peaks, until the mountains themselves seemed to roar with fury and rage at the intruders that had disturbed their peace. Glancing back over her shoulder Clara saw that the rearing, bulging slopes of the mountains had subtly altered to form a huge, almost human shape. It was as though an enormous giant was moving with great lumbering steps behind her.

"I saw him!" she screamed. "Lord Rothlan, I saw him! The Old Man of the Mountains! He's behind us!"

Fully alert to the danger, the horses frantically lengthened their stride as the mountains lurched dangerously close, their steep sides shedding tumbling boulders that bounced in great, jarring leaps towards them. Guiding the horses in their desperate, headlong flight, Rothlan peered ahead and his heart contracted as he saw that, even as the sea loomed nearer, the valley in front of them was steadily narrowing. Their escape was being cut off.

Huge rocks were now crashing around them but the magic in their cloaks protected them and even boulders that seemed ready to bounce straight onto them were somehow deflected and fell to one side.

"Keep together," the Ranger shouted, for he could see the danger of rocks landing between the feet of the horses and if one of them were to fall, it would, he knew, be the end of them.

As the mountains heaved about them, the sea now glinted tantalizingly close. To their horror, however, the gap between the two mountains seemed to be swelling upwards as well as inwards, threatening to bar their way completely and at each side the slopes bulged ever closer until they found themselves confined to a narrow passageway.

They barely noticed the thin mist that wafted gently from the hillside but as they rode through it, they felt a dreadful tiredness seeping through them as though their last reserves of energy were being drained from them. Rothlan paled as he felt the deadly effects of the spell that was enveloping them and fervently hoped that the horses would have enough strength left to clear the valley. It was the thought of the horrific damage that the boulders would cause if they smashed the horses' wings that made him leave his order until the very last moment.

"*Serai*," he called out sharply. The horses' wings immediately sprang forth and as the black horses of Ruksh lifted off the ground to soar to safety through the frighteningly thin sliver of light that remained between the hills, the mountain slopes crashed angrily together behind them.

Relief washed over them as they saw the sea below and ahead, on a distant shore, the grim bulk of a huge castle.

Inveraray Castle, the stronghold of the Clan Campbell.

22. Amgarad Attacks

The smartly-suited delegation from the Scottish Fishermen's Federation approached the French Consulate looking so utterly respectable that the police constables on guard were easily overpowered and had their weapons and radios removed before they realized what was going on. Even as they were manhandled down the steps, a white van pulled up in front of the consulate with a screech of brakes and as its back doors were flung open, the hapless constables were swiftly bundled inside.

Inside the consulate, Amgarad raised his head sharply as a shrill whistle from the street was followed by the pounding of feet as hundreds of furious fishermen seemed to appear from nowhere. It was, thought Jimmie Leadbetter, a very well-planned operation and stage one had been completed successfully. He saw the consul at the window and grinned malevolently at him.

A huge crowd of fishermen now filled the street and there was a massive cheer as a couple of young lads tore the Tricouleur from its flagpole and threw it to the ground. As the French flag blazed on the cobbles, a select band of the strongest and toughest fishermen surged heavily against the door of the building. Leadbetter urged them on. "Take it down, boys," he shouted encouragingly.

Inside the consulate, the count fumed with rage as his terrified staff hovered in the hall and looked to him for instructions. The roars of anger from the other side of the door were frightening and two of the secretaries were already showing signs of hysteria.

"Take the staff up to the first floor, Pierre," he instructed, "and put every moveable object you can find across the stairs to make a barricade. I don't know where the police are but I can tell you one thing for sure ... they're not outside our front door at the moment!"

As the main door was showing signs of cracking off its hinges, the count went into his office and hastily put every document he could find in the safe and shut the massive door with the keys inside. Looking at his handiwork in satisfaction he turned and smiled shakily at the little grouse.

The count was under no misapprehension as to the danger he was in and he knew that if the mob got into the consulate then the best he could hope for was a bad beating; the worst, he did not care to think about. The sound of the door coming off its hinges made him realize that it was too late to give the little grouse to any of the staff upstairs.

"Come on," he muttered, scanning the room swiftly, "let's put you somewhere safe." Two wall vases filled with flowers and trailing ivy decorated the wall on either side of the official French Seal and pulling a chair forward he stood on it and quickly stuffed Amgarad behind some carnations.

"Don't move," he instructed.

By the time the fishermen burst in, brandishing clubs and baseball bats, the count was once again sitting calmly behind his desk, his heart beating uncomfortably fast. The noise was tremendous as they piled into the room in a roar of sound. Louis de Charillon, however, was no coward. He paled visibly but his chin rose determinedly.

"Gentlemen?" he enquired icily, bracing himself for the attack as they surged furiously towards him.

Suddenly, as though someone had pressed the pause button on a film clip, they froze in a strange, quivering tableau in front of him, cudgels raised to strike.

The count looked at them blankly and watched in amazement as the violence drained from their contorted faces to be replaced by a cringing look of utter terror. Fear, horror and dread shone in their eyes and the brave leaders of the pack, who had entered the room ready and willing to assault an unarmed man, now seemed to be shrinking back against those pushing from behind.

It was then that he realized that they were not actually looking at him at all — they were staring, horrified and appalled, at something behind him!

De Charillon swung round in his chair and gasped in amazement. It was as though the eagle in the French Seal had come to life; for perched on top of it, wings outstretched and neck thrust aggressively forward, was the most enormous eagle the count had ever seen.

Impressive at the best of times, Amgarad used every ounce of magic he possessed to induce total dread in the now terrified fishermen; for he was furiously angry at the attack on the defenceless consul.

To the horror of the crowd, he launched himself over the consul's head, straight at them; his terrifying scream of rage reducing them to total panic. Cudgels were dropped as they covered their heads with their arms to protect themselves from his razor-sharp beak and vicious talons.

The screaming crowd now turned and fought its way back through the press of people still trying to come in and, a few minutes later, as police cars, sirens blaring, came shrieking round the corner, the amazed policemen found a street crowded by milling hordes of terrified men. Amgarad's spell still held them in a thrall of fear and several were shaking uncontrollably after their terrifying ordeal. Some grasped the policemen's arms as they climbed out of their cars, demanding protection and babbling incoherently about a huge eagle.

By the time the policemen entered the hall, however, there was no sign of an eagle, either inside or out. They found the consul still looking slightly dazed and, realizing that he was in a state of shock, treated him gently. With the arrival of the police, his staff moved the chairs and tables they had used as a barricade and ventured tentatively downstairs, wondering if they had imagined the sight of the enormous eagle that had so effectively dealt with the riot.

De Charillon, however, knew in his heart that he would never see it again; for before the police had arrived, he had frantically pulled a chair to the wall and searched through the flowers for his little grouse.

It had gone, and all that remained to show that it had ever been there, were a few, very small, brown feathers.

23. Inveraray Castle

The sentries on the walls of Inveraray Castle had never known a day like it. Even Kitor, perched on a handy buttress of the castle, couldn't believe his eyes. He'd been hanging around Inveraray all day, waiting with increasing anxiety for the riders to appear — but never had he expected them to arrive like this!

The dreadful thunder from Hell's Glen had carried clearly across the waters of the loch and within minutes had brought every inmate of the castle to its walls. From his perch, Kitor listened with interest to what they said and, if the truth be told, found it hard to believe, for tales of the Old Man of the Mountains had long since passed into legend. But the sight of hordes of tartan-clad clansmen crowding the battlements, looking at one another with terror in their hearts, infected him with a feeling of acute unease and soon he, too, was watching in petrified wonder to see what would happen next.

Nothing, however, had prepared them for the sight of the beautiful winged horses that soared from amid the tumbling, crashing mountains; a detail, Kitor noted sourly, that the prince had omitted to mention! Any fear among the watchers on the battlements that they might be an attacking force was short-lived as everyone was quick to notice that the horses seemed to be faltering and, as they came closer, were dropping lower and lower towards the waters of the loch as their great wings lost their strength.

"They're never going to make it, master! They're going to fall into the loch!" an alarmed Captain of the Guard spoke respectfully to Archibald Campbell, Chieftain of the Clan Campbell, as he joined him on the battlements.

Indeed, it was obvious that the horses were tiring with every flap of their wings and although they were struggling bravely to stay in the air, it was still uncertain if they would make it to the safety of land. The crowd of villagers that had gathered at the edge of the loch, held their breaths as, one by one, the horses managed to reach the shore, splashing heavily into the shallow water. Absolutely exhausted, they then collapsed onto their knees in the sand, wings outspread and chests heaving. A great cheer arose as the crowd pressed forward to get a better view of the horses and their riders but, despite their interest, they took care not to venture too close.

"Help Lord Rothlan, Dad," Neil urged as he swung his legs over Chakra's back and splashed across to Jaikie and Hamish who had both fallen over the necks of their horses. He could tell from their heavy breathing that they weren't dead but he didn't want them to slide off and topple into the water. He looked at Clara who was half carrying Lady Ellan up the beach and managed to drag Hamish clear of the waves before grabbing Jaikie under the arms and hauling him clear of the lapping water.

Lord Rothlan, clinging heavily to the Ranger was, at least, still on his feet but he looked like death warmed up. "Are you ... all right, Ranger?" he asked, his words slow and slurred.

The Ranger nodded. "We seem to be fine, thank heavens, but you look as though you could sleep for a week! What happened? Was it a spell?"

Rothlan nodded. "So ... tired," he muttered, looking anxiously at his horse. "Take the magic crystal from my saddlebag. Take it now and don't give it to anyone, do you understand? I must tell the MacArthur ..." he swayed on his feet, "I must tell the MacArthur . . . what has happened."

"Get the crystal, Neil," the Ranger said, catching Lord Rothlan as his knees buckled under him, "and don't let anyone see what it is. Hide it under your cloak."

To distract the gathering crowd's attention, he beckoned to a burly man wrapped in a plaid of the Campbell tartan. "Hey, you! Give me a hand here!" he called. The man's reaction was to cross himself fervently and stay firmly where he was. It was only when Archibald Campbell himself came to the shore that litters were brought and Rothlan, Lady Ellan, Hamish and Jaikie were lifted onto them and taken up to the castle.

"You stay with Lady Ellan, Clara," said the Ranger quietly, taking charge. "And Neil, you stay with Rothlan. Try to keep him awake long enough to use the crystal. We'll have to have help from the hill! And tell him I'll see that the horses are properly stabled."

The horses had managed to pull themselves shakily to their feet and, much to the amazement of the watchers, had drawn back their wings. The Ranger moved towards Rothlan's horse and stroked its neck gently. "Come on, Rasta, old fellow," he murmured. "Where you go, the rest will follow!" He led them in procession through the houses of the village to the towering walls of the castle and the stables where grooms were already laying straw for the magnificent animals.

The chief of the Clan Campbell, overwhelmed by the arrival of people who obviously came from another world, was seriously worried; his concern only mitigated by the fact that they seemed badly in need of his help. Nevertheless, he did not quite know what to make of his unexpected guests. "Why would they come here?" he remarked to his wife while they were upstairs, dressing for dinner. "We've nothing to offer them. Our cattle are diseased and our harvest this year has been thin. And to travel on flying horses ... they must be magicians."

"Of course, they're magicians," his wife said sharply, "that's obvious. How else could they have such horses? And what were they doing in Hell's Glen?"

"They were lucky to get out alive, Agnes. Who would have thought that the Old Man of the Mountain still exists?"

"Yes, but many others have ventured into Hell's Glen over the years and the mountains haven't risen against them," she pointed out. "Whoever they are, they must indeed be powerful to have roused the Old Man of the Mountains; especially the one they call Lord Rothlan."

Archie Campbell nodded. "He's sick," he said. "From what I saw of him, he might well not last the night. There's nothing wrong with the man or his children but the others, the small ones ..." He frowned as he looked in the mirror and adjusted the ruffles at the neck of his shirt, "they might not be magicians but they're magic people, all the same."

"You would be wise to be careful in your dealings with them, Archie," Agnes cautioned, her voice serious. "It won't do to displease them and, who knows, one day we might want a favour returned!"

Archibald Campbell nodded his head in agreement. "Aye, that's true," he said. "But the sooner they leave Inveraray, the happier I'll be!"

In a bedroom in another wing of the castle, Neil barred the door as Lord Rothlan, propped up by pillows in a four-poster bed of enormous proportions, gazed wearily into his crystal and concentrated what was left of his mind on calling Archie.

As the crystal in the hill glowed with light, Archie moved forward to peer into its depths. He took one look at Rothlan's face and called the MacArthur.

"They're in trouble," he said abruptly. "Rothlan can hardly keep his eyes open so you'd better be quick! It seems that he got caught up with the old Man of the Mountains!"

"Cri'achan Mor?" the MacArthur looked surprised.

"Rothlan's caught in one of his spells, by the look of it."

"Did you tell him that Amgarad is back?"

"No, I didn't. I thought you'd like to give him the good news," Archie smiled, moving over so that the MacArthur could take his place.

"Alasdair, listen to me," the MacArthur began, "Amgarad is back in the hill and I am going to send him to you. He will bring firestones with him so that you can counteract the spell."

Rothlan gave a shaky smile. "Good ... news! What happened at the consulate?"

"The fishermen attacked it but Amgarad managed to sort them out. The consul's fine, don't worry."

"Sir James?"

"He's helping me just now with a wee scheme I have in mind. You relax — I'll keep in touch!"

Lord Rothlan looked at Neil over the top of the crystal. "Amgarad is coming," he whispered in relief. "Tell Lady Ellan. He's bringing firestones. We'll be okay!"

24. Number Ten

Given the prospect of a rift with Scotland and imminent war with France, the British Prime Minister was, one way or another, having a bad week and in all fairness could be excused a smidgeon of bad temper. It is also true that the flurry of seriously-worded, top-secret communiqués that had crossed her desk with alarming frequency that day had done little to prepare her for faery tales and, as she listened with blank amazement to Charles Wyndham's ramblings about dragons and crystal balls, it was hardly surprising that she threw a wobbly of mammoth proportions. Never one to suffer fools gladly, she came close to shredding the head of MI5 where he stood.

"Have – you – gone – out – of – your – mind, Charles?" she demanded, her voice cracking with disbelief.

Sir Charles Wyndham heaved a sigh and eyed her in much the same way as he would a prowling tiger. He had known that this was going to be a particularly sticky interview.

"I know it sounds utterly and completely incredible, Prime Minister," he said evenly, "and my reaction was exactly the same as yours when I first heard it." He paused uncertainly and tried for a little lightness of touch. "I really thought old Tatler had gone round the bend, to tell you the truth."

"Are you seriously trying to tell me that in a time of grave danger to the nation we should defend ourselves with ..." she was loath to pronounce the word, "... faeries?"

"I think we could do worse than give them a sporting chance!"

Now completely convinced that he was barking mad, her voice rose by a couple of octaves. "A sporting chance?" she repeated, incredulously. "Sir Charles, may I remind you that you hold one of the top offices in government. When I receive a report from you, I most certainly do not expect a lot of ... of drivel about faeries! Do I make myself clear?"

It didn't take an IQ of 145 plus (and Sir Charles's IQ was much, much higher than that) to read the Prime Minister's mind.

"I'm as sane as you are PM," he observed with a shaky smile, "and believe me, despite the fact that my department doesn't believe in faeries on principle, I am now quite convinced that they really do exist." He took a deep breath, wondering just how much to tell her. Better, perhaps, to leave out the bit about magic carpets. She'd think he'd gone completely round the bend if he told her that. "Tatler took me to visit them. They're called the MacArthurs. I've seen them and spoken to them and I'm quite convinced that they can get us out of this mess with the French."

The Prime Minister looked at him in utter amazement and shook her head. Things couldn't get much worse than this! The man was obviously a lunatic!

"Charles," she spoke in tones normally reserved for errant five-year olds, "the French not only have a fleet of trawlers in the North Sea, they also have a fleet of warships! You are wasting my time!"

Sir Charles threw out his hands in protest. "Do you think I don't realize the gravity of the situation, Prime Minister? I'm just as worried as you are, for goodness sake! Look," he bent over her desk and brought his face close to hers, "you've known me for years now. Have I ever let you down before? Do you really think I'd waste your time with a load of childish rubbish if it weren't true?"

Something in his expression suddenly made her bite back the scathing retort that had sprung to her lips and he relaxed imperceptibly as he saw her expression change. Indeed, her face was a picture as she struggled to believe the unbelievable. "But, you can't mean ..." she whispered, "you can't mean that ... it *is* true?"

Sir Charles almost smiled. "Oh yes, my dear Prime Minister, it's true all right! And I can prove it! That's why I had to see you so urgently."

He placed a black box on her desk. "This is what they gave me when I visited Arthur's Seat," he said lifting the lid carefully and easing a glittering crystal ball from its velvet depths. "I know it takes a bit of swallowing at first but I promise you, Prime Minister, it's the real thing. *And,*" he said in a whisper tinged with heart-stopping elation, *"it's ours to keep!"*

The Prime Minister's mind leapt at the thought and, as their eyes met in heady anticipation of the days and events to come, he pressed a firestone into her hand. He'd already threaded a chain through it. "Wear it round your neck, Prime Minister," he instructed, "and you'll be able to activate the crystal. Like this."

Sir Charles passed his hand over the crystal and as it glowed into life, she saw the MacArthur sitting on his great chair with a fearsome, red dragon curled at his feet.

The MacArthur and the Prime Minister talked for nearly half an hour and by the end of their conversation, the Prime Minster's face had lost its drawn, haggard look and a glimmer of hope lurked in her eyes.

"But ... will it work?" she stared at him, suddenly desperate for reassurance. "Can ... I mean, are you sure you can do it?"

"It'll work, never fear!" the MacArthur said confidently.

At this assurance, a slow smile crossed the Prime Minister's face as, like Tatler, she visualized the effect it would have on the French.

The conversation finished, Wyndham watched the crystal mist over and, picking it up, replaced it carefully in its box, eyeing her with a mixture of curiosity and relief as she flung herself back in her chair.

He raised his eyebrows. "Well, Prime Minister?" he queried, somewhat archly.

Her customary, stern expression suddenly slipped and disintegrated into what he could only describe as gleeful grin as she threw out her hands helplessly at the complete absurdity of the situation.

"This is all *totally* unbelievable," she said, shaking her head as she reached for the telephone, "and heaven alone knows *what* the Admiralty is going to say when I tell them to stand the fleet down."

Charles Wyndham, who had a fairly good idea of what the Admiralty would say, rubbed his chin as his lips creased in a knowing smile. His eyes twinkled.

"Go for it, Prime Minister," he advised.

25. The Road to Appin

Clara looked at the towering range of mountains that stretched as far as the distant horizon and her heart plummeted at the thought of having to cross them all. She might have felt slightly better about it had the day been bright and sunny but, as it happened, it had rained ever since they'd left Inveraray. Amgarad circled in the sky and she waved and raised a smile as he came to fly beside her. Cheer up, she told herself, as the steadily beating wings of the flying horses took them over more mountain peaks; at least the dreadful spell has been lifted and Amgarad is with us.

They had all worried about Lord Rothlan who had slept soundly until Amgarad had arrived with the firestones and restored him to health. Lady Ellan had told her that she suspected that the spell cast by the Old Man of the Mountains had been aimed at him alone as the others had all recovered and been up and about after a very short space of time; even the horses had regained their strength by the following morning.

And it hadn't been at all bad at Inveraray for the Campbell chief had done his best to entertain them during their brief stay. Indeed, when Lord Rothlan had recovered, he had held a great feast for them. Afterwards there had been a ceilidh but although the celebrations had, by the sound of it, continued until morning, the travellers had nevertheless taken to their beds well before midnight so that they could make an early start. The first stage of their journey over the mountains, Rothlan had told them, would be the longest, for Campbell had drawn rolls of maps from the shelves of his library and shown him the paths that the raiders used to move quickly through the glens.

Now, thank goodness, Lord Rothlan was his normal self and delighted to have Amgarad with him. Clara smiled. Seeing Amgarad again had cheered them all considerably and they'd listened fascinated to his story of how the Scottish fishermen had attacked the French consulate and been forced into undignified flight.

Inveraray Castle, however, now lay far behind them and although flying on the winged horses was exciting; she half-wished that their journey were over. When she thought of how they were going to steal into Prince Kalman's castle and take the crown, however, she quickly revised her opinion. Maybe it was just as well that the journey *hadn't* yet finished. She wasn't ready for the scary part that lay ahead and the magic words the Sultan had given her seemed to be hidden deep in her mind. What would happen, she worried, if she couldn't remember them when the time came to say them?

Lunch that day was an uncomfortable meal by the side of a stream that gurgled down the mountainside. The rain was steady and the rocks that flanked the stream gleamed wet and shiny against the sparse grass. Clara thought she caught a movement out of the corner of her eye and looked round sharply but there was nothing there. She thought of the crow that had followed them to Loch Lomond and wondered if it had somehow found them. She'd ask Amgarad to keep an eye open for it.

As it happened, Amgarad's arrival at Inveraray had been a severe shock to Kitor. So much so, that he'd taken half an hour to stop shaking. It had been the last thing he'd expected, for until then he hadn't had a clue as to who the riders actually were. Lord Rothlan and Amgarad! He sweated with fear as he realized the quality of the opposition lined up against him, for when he had been looking for the crown in Jarishan Loch, Kalman's fear of Rothlan had told the wily crow that he was a magician to be reckoned with.

Although driven by terror of the prince, however, Kitor was not without courage and even as he wondered dismally how long he could survive against such odds, he nevertheless continued to slip warily round the castle, listening to conversations among the clansmen to find out what was going on.

As the main topic of conversation revolved round the travellers it did not take him long to find out that Archie Campbell was in his library with Lord Rothlan and, as luck would have it, he fluttered onto a window-ledge while they were discussing the secret routes that wound through the mountains to Appin. He listened greedily to what was being said and that evening, when the prince had spoken to him through the crystal, had immediately passed on all of his information.

Kitor's tale of the travellers' dramatic arrival in Inveraray, however, did not meet with quite the praise he'd expected. There was a shade of anger and disappointment in Kalman's voice when he heard of the happenings in Hell's Glen that told the astute crow that his master had probably had a hand in awakening the Old Man of the Mountain. Yes, he pondered, the prince had expected to hear very different news from him that evening.

Nevertheless, he knew by the tone of his voice that the prince was pleased to hear details of the route the riders were going to follow. Pleased and relieved

— and considerate, too, for he had told him of the cave in which he was now resting. It was sheltered from the wind by a jutting buttress of rock and perched so high on the mountain that he could see for miles across the rain-swept landscape. He fluffed his feathers contentedly, proud at having been of such assistance to his master. Comfortably placed to keep watch for the little group as it made its way towards Appin, he was able to report sighting them on the first day of their journey.

"Are you sure?" demanded the prince. "How can they have travelled so far already?"

"Master," Kitor perched on a spur of rock just inside the entrance to the cave, "master, they are not riding through the valleys; they are flying on the winged horses from peak to peak. By tomorrow they will surely reach Appin and your castle at Ardray."

Kitor heard the prince hiss in fury. "They will never reach Ardray, Kitor. Watch carefully and you will see how I deal with my enemies!"

The beam of light that held him in the sight of the crystal faded and, knowing that the prince was no longer watching him, the crow fluttered to the lip of the cave to see what would happen to the little group. Perhaps, he thought, they might be blown up by thunderbolts or perhaps the prince might destroy the flying horses in mid-flight. Nothing, however, prepared him for what was happening. He gasped in pure horror for, even as he watched, the sky was changing from dull grey to a deep, dark brown and the wind was rising, blowing violent, purple clouds across the mountains. His eyes sharpened as he glimpsed them in the skirts of the clouds; shapes and forms that he had only ever heard tell of in legends of old. Riding the wind on broomsticks, black hair flying and cloaks

swirling, they swooped, revelling in their unaccustomed freedom across the length and breadth of the
heavens.

"Snow witches!" Kitor stared at them in awful fascination and marvelled at his master's power.

26. Snow Witches

Lord Rothlan looked up as the clouds started to swirl and darken and saw the snow witches on their broomsticks at much the same time as Kitor.

"Snow witches," he called to Lady Ellan, who had immediately flown up beside him and was staring in horror at the sky around her.

"I've heard of them," she called back, "but I never thought to see them. This is the prince's work for sure!"

"We must land at once," Rothlan said, pulling at Rasta's reins. "Quickly, follow me, everyone!" The winged horses slipped into line behind him as he headed downwards towards the winding track that they had been following through the mountains.

Once on firm ground, Neil and Clara loosened the horses' reins and sat gaping in open-mouthed wonder as they watched the witches soar and swoop on the wind like darting shoals of fish, their eerie, screaming cries echoing weirdly over the mountains. The clouds fused and melted in an evil jumble of hideous colour before their eyes and, even as they watched, the first few flakes of snow drifted through the sky.

"How many of them are there?" Ellan asked, her eyes scanning the swirling clouds.

"Hundreds!" Rothlan snapped.

"What'll we do?" the Ranger asked, looking around anxiously as the first snowflakes, large and white, started to fall softly around them.

Lord Rothlan came to a swift decision. "We'll have to split up," he said, scanning the sky as Amgarad swooped in to perch on his shoulder. "You must protect the children, Ranger; whatever happens, they must get through to Ardray, for only they know the magic words. Now, listen carefully," he said, gathering them around him, "the snow witches cast spells that freeze their victims but the Sultan's cloaks will protect us from their hexes as well as from the cold. Even the horses have a built-in magic that will protect them. While Jaikie, Hamish and I keep them busy, you must try to slip unseen across the mountains. It's not far now and you'll be all right as long as you follow the track. If the blizzard gets too bad, try to find shelter — a cave or something. In the meantime, we'll try to draw off the witches."

The witches, now swooping here and there across the slopes of the mountains, were searching for them everywhere; their screeching calls echoing through the air. The snow was becoming thicker and, nodding to Hamish and Jaikie to do the same, Rothlan quickly eased his saddlebags from his horse's back. "You'd better take these," he said to the children. "They'll only hinder us in the air and we'll need every bit of mobility we've got if we're going to outwit that little lot."

As Neil and Clara hurriedly slung the bags over the necks of their horses, Rothlan fumbled in his saddle bag and drew out his crystal. "Take this, Ellan," he said urgently, putting it into her outstretched hands, "and let your father know what is happening. Our journey is no longer a secret," he looked grimly at the snow witches, "Kalman seems to know our every move! Take care, my dear." He gripped her hands in his but his last words, spoken softly, were whipped away by the wind. Then, with a final wave, Lord Rothlan turned his horse towards the screaming hordes of witches. "Ready, Hamish? Jaikie?" he looked at them both and smiled encouragingly. "Come on, then! Let's go!" The order rang out. "*Serai!*" they called together. The horses' wings grew in seconds and, in no time at all, the three riders had flapped strongly upwards into the swirl of falling snowflakes, with Amgarad soaring above them.

"It's not going to be that easy," Neil predicted as he strained his eyes to follow them. "The witches have scattered and the snow is getting thicker!"

The Ranger looked worried and glanced at Lady Ellan whose eyes were still following the riders in the sky. She smiled shakily as she turned back to the little group but her voice was calm as she spoke hurriedly to Neil and Clara. "Wrap your cloaks around you," she told them, "and keep a firm hold on the reins in case the horses slip. This is only the beginning; the snow is going to get a lot worse!"

Clara pulled the hood of her cloak over her head and wrapped its comfortable folds round her. Despite the cold, the cloak gave her a wonderful feeling of warmth and safety. Encased in its gentle glow, she draped as much of it as she could over Sephia's flanks as she knew that the horse would find it easier to travel if warm and dry.

When Ellan finished telling her father of the appearance of the snow witches, she stowed the crystal safely back in her saddlebag and, seeing that they were all ready and waiting, led the way forward. The snow was now falling in thick, heavy flakes which showed no sign of easing and, as the drifts deepened, the track disappeared and landmarks that might have helped them find their way were blotted out under the glaring whiteness of the snow. Nevertheless, they made steady progress at first as the trail was wide and followed the side of the mountain but, as they penetrated deeper into the hills, it soon became apparent that they were lost when, instead of following an even trail, the horses found themselves scrambling between outcrops of rock.

As the blizzard thickened, Lady Ellan called a halt. "I'm afraid to go any further," she told the Ranger. "We're totally lost and I can't see a thing in front of me apart from the snow. I don't want the horses to lose their footing and break their legs on these rocks or maybe slip down a sheer drop by mistake."

By this time, they were all layered in snow. Neil looked like a snowman and, realizing the weight of snow that the horses were carrying, Clara turned Sephia to the side of the track and shook her cloak to get rid of it all.

A sudden swooshing sound in the air made them freeze in their saddles. A coven of snow witches had spotted them through the driving blizzard. Screaming in triumph, they bore down on the little group and their leader, using her broom like a battering ram, headed straight for Lady Ellan, knocking her off Rihan's back, into the snow.

In the seconds that the snowflakes parted to allow the witches to fly unhindered through the blizzard, Clara had a clear view of the sky beyond and what she saw filled her heart with dread; for Amgarad, wings outstretched, was toppling out of the sky, spiralling downwards and making no attempt to fly.

Clara didn't think twice. *"Serai!"* she snapped. Sephia's wings grew in an instant and she immediately took off into the blizzard; for she, too, had seen the falling eagle and, flapping her wings strongly, headed straight for it.

As Lady Ellan struggled to rise from the snowdrift, the witches zoomed triumphantly amongst them and, with jubilant screams, threw their spells. Much to their astonishment, however, they had no effect. Thoroughly alarmed, they watched open-mouthed as the hexes bounced off the riders' cloaks and proceeded to zig-zag harmlessly among the rocks. Lady Ellan, rising from the snowdrift, took in the situation at a glance and before the witches realized what was happening, straightened her arm and hexed witch after witch in quick flashes of blistering light.

The Ranger, still stunned at the swiftness of the attack, dismounted and picking his way round the bodies of the witches, reached out a hand to help Lady Ellan who was floundering in the deep snow. "Are you all right?" he asked, grasping her arm and hauling her to her feet.

Breathing heavily, she shook the snow off her hair and cloak and dusted herself down. "Yes, yes, thank you, Ranger. I'm fine."

"You were wonderful, Lady Ellan," Neil said with respect. "I didn't know you could hex people like that!"

"Fortunately I don't have to do it too often, Neil," she smiled, "but from now on, we'll have to keep a care-ful look-out. They took me completely by surprise."

They looked down in silence at the crumpled figure of one of the witches. The flowing, layered silks of her dress were the ivory of the clouds, her cloak a wonder of shredded lengths of delicate, silvery chiffon and her face, under the drooping, pointed hat, was framed by long ear-flaps of braided, silver ribbons. It was her face that captured their attention, however, for the witch was beautiful. Long black hair curled round a face that was pale and breathtakingly lovely.

"She ... she's beautiful!" the Ranger exclaimed in surprise. "I always thought witches were ugly, old crones!"

Lady Ellan smiled grimly. "Don't judge by appearances, Ranger. She has eyes of stone and for all her beauty, her heart is as black as the night! Take my word for it!"

Neil walked over to where her broomstick lay and picked it up. He felt magic tingle through him as he did so and looked quickly at Lady Ellan.

"I can feel the magic in it," he said. "Is it all right for me to hold it?"

"Let me see it?" Ellan took it from him and looked at it carefully.

Neil continued. "I noticed when they flew in, that there were empty spaces round them. I mean, no snowflakes were landing on the witches at all. If we each held a broomstick out in front of us then perhaps we could see where we were going." He looked round at the broomsticks, scattered here and there in the snow. "There are more than enough, Lady Ellan. We could sling them on either side of the horses." He looked round, his eyes scanning the sky. "In fact, I think we might have to for, if anything, the blizzard is getting worse!"

It was then that they missed Clara. So alarmed had everyone been at the witches' ferocious attack that no one had noticed that she had gone. Neil ran back down the track holding a broomstick in front of him to clear the driving snow, but despite being able to see for quite a distance, there was no sign of Clara or her horse.

"I don't understand this at all!" Ellan stated, shaking her head in disbelief. "I saw nothing when I was in the snow but you *must* have noticed if they took Clara, surely?"

"She dropped behind me," Neil said. "I didn't see anything. And if they did take her, then where's Sephia?"

Lady Ellan looked at the Ranger and read the despair in his eyes. "Whatever has happened, we must go on, John, and hope that she finds us again. We can't go back! Remember, nothing can happen to her; she is under the Sultan's protection."

Sick with worry, Neil looked at his father and nodded. "Lady Ellan's right, Dad. We have to go on."

Neil gathered the broomsticks that lay stuck at various angles in the snowdrifts and passed them to his father who tied them lengthwise along the sides of their saddles under the horses' harnesses. Lady Ellan breathed a sigh of relief as she realized that Neil had been right; they *did* make a difference. The snow around her had disappeared and she could now see ahead for quite a considerable distance.

The Ranger, grim-faced and tight-lipped, mounted his horse with a heavy heart and was just about to urge it forward when they heard the scream of snow witches again. Freezing where they stood, they peered fearfully into the whirling white flakes.

Neil's sudden exclamation of joy at seeing Sephia loom out of the blizzard was cut short as he saw that the horse was being harassed by two snow witches who soared and swooped round the desperate animal, trying vainly to hex it out of the sky.

Lady Ellan moved quickly. Urging her horse forward, she straightened her arm and as a streak of light shot from her fingers, one of the witches slumped forward with a scream of agony and fell before them. The second witch tried to flee but she had left it too late and even as she swung her broomstick round, a hex hit her and she too, tumbled out of the sky and fell, cloak and skirts swirling crazily, into a nearby drift.

It was only when Sephia landed that joy changed to horror, for they saw then that the horse had no rider and Lady Ellan gave an anguished cry as, grasping Sephia's bridle she saw, lying awkwardly over the saddle, the stiff body of an eagle.

It was Amgarad. The witches had frozen him with one of their spells.

27. Kalman's Captive

So desperately worried was she at Amgarad's plight that Clara hadn't actually realized that no one had seen her leave. As she flew through the blizzard, she tried to catch sight of the falling bird; for apart from that first dreadful glimpse, she had not been able to see him again as the snowflakes, whirling dizzily round her head, blotted out everything else. Sephia, however, being a magic horse, had the advantage. Flying faster than she had ever done before, she had immediately homed in on Amgarad and knew exactly where he was as he fell through the air. Lower and lower she swooped until Clara was afraid they might hit the ground. Nevertheless, she had the sense to give the horse its head as it seemed so confident in its flight. Then she saw Amgarad, still dropping like a stone and, as Sephia flew alongside, she reached out and caught his wing. It was as stiff as a board. With a scream of horror, she pulled the great eagle over the saddle and caught the frozen bird in her arms just as the ground loomed beneath them.

"Amgarad," she cried in anguish. "Amgarad!"

Sephia landed on a flat rock beside a rushing stream that ran black between banks piled high with snow. Clara, tears streaming down her cheeks, was totally grief-stricken. Was Amgarad dead, she wondered, or could her magic cloak melt the ice that held his feathers so stiff and unbending?

Above her, she could hear the witches shrieking but the snow was so thick that she could see nothing. If only she could find Lord Rothlan, she was sure he would be able to bring Amgarad back to life. But how much time did she have?

"Oh, Amgarad," she cried, pressing her cheek against his head, "we must save you."

"Hurry Clara," Sephia whinnied, tossing her head warningly as the witches came closer and fear clutched at Clara's heart as she looked up and scanned the whirling snowflakes. She knew that to save Amgarad she had to get him back to Lady Ellan.

"Fly Sephia," she whispered urgently.

They were only in the air for a few minutes before the witches appeared. Even as Sephia soared upwards they screamed down out of the blizzard and fear ran through her as she felt their hexes bouncing off her cloak.

"Look out, Clara!" Sephia shrilled the warning as one of the witches swooped and tried to use her broomstick as a battering ram. Clara ducked just in time but felt the touch of the witch's cloak as she screamed past and then saw that a second witch was zooming in on her. Desperately, she wedged Amgarad's frozen body between the high pommels of Sephia's saddle. There were so many witches and she was helpless to save herself.

"Go to Lady Ellan, Sephia," she screamed as the witch's broomstick hit her hard in the back and knocked her out of the saddle.

Cloak billowing behind her, she felt herself falling through the air but did not have time to feel frightened as a snow witch, with a cry of triumph, looped swiftly underneath her and caught her firmly. Suddenly the air seemed full of snow witches, all shrieking victoriously.

Clara automatically grasped the handle of the broomstick to keep her balance and stared around fearfully. No snow fell on her and she gasped with amazement as she realized that the witches travelled in a bubble of clear air. It was the first time that she had been close to them and she gasped at how beautiful they were. Bracing herself, she turned to look at the witch that sat behind her and immediately wished that she hadn't; for the beautiful face set in its frame of glittering, silver ribbons, had eyes of stone.

Clara felt sick at the sight of her and turning round quickly, gripped the broomstick tightly in trembling hands.

Where *are* they taking me, she wondered fearfully, for the witches were no longer careering haphazardly round the sky. They were flying in a straight line and had, it seemed, a definite destination. She began to wonder if they might be taking her back to their lair when, through the snow, she saw they were heading for the massive, rocky peaks of a high mountain and, as they drew closer, saw the dark mouth of a cave, set in a sheer cliff.

Kitor watched the witches approach and his eyes gleamed as he saw their captive. But had they caught the right child? He shifted on his claws and fluttered to the edge of the cave to receive the witches. They had done well, he thought, fluffing his feathers. His master was going to be very pleased indeed.

The cave was no more than a hole in the cliff. It was so small that Clara could just stand up in it without bumping her head on its rocky ceiling.

"Make yourself comfortable," invited the black crow, who had told her his name was Kitor.

Clara drew her cloak around her and cleared stones and loose bits of rock to one side so that she could lean against the side of the cave. The dazzlingly beautiful witches in their robes of flowing gauze had dumped her unceremoniously at the edge of the cave and, given the drop to the valley below, she had been quick to scramble inside. Kitor had bowed and scraped before the witches and she'd watched them leave with mixed feelings. What was going to happen to her now?

Not a lot, seemed to be the answer to that question. The cave was small, stony and cold and, apart from Kitor, contained nothing. Clara was glad of her cloak, for its warmth gave her comfort. She sat huddled in its soft folds and worried. She worried about Amgarad and Sephia and hoped they had made it back to the others. And had Lord Rothlan returned? Would he be able to save Amgarad? Her mind went round and round in circles until, worn out by worry, exhaustion and the excitement of the past hours, the magic of the cloak overcame her fears. She found her eyes closing and, despite the hardness of the floor, curled herself into a ball and fell fast asleep.

28. The Storm Carriers

The problem was, thought Lord Rothlan, that there were just too many witches. The more witches he hexed, the more they seemed to multiply until the air around him whirled with as many witches as there were snowflakes. Glancing across the sky, he could see that both Hamish and Jaikie were up against much the same thing and although witches were falling out of the sky around them, there were always more to take their place. Grimly, he pulled on his horse's reins to keep close to them as it would be madness to let themselves be separated. The only thing that gave him comfort was that his tactics were working and he was steadily drawing the witches away from Lady Ellan, giving her time to travel deeper into the mountains.

Desperately, he kept the witches' attention so that they wouldn't give up for they must be able to see that their spells were having little effect and, indeed, their hexes were bouncing all over the sky. And where was Amgarad? He kept hoping to catch a glimpse of him but the snow and the witches made it difficult to see anything.

It was then that the Queen of the Witches soared into view. Her beauty took his breath away. Never had he seen a more beautiful woman. Unafraid of his hexes, she sailed close to him and held her broomstick in the air by his side. Dimly he was conscious that Jaikie and Hamish had brought their horses up close and were flying just behind him.

"It would grieve me to have to kill you, Lord Rothlan," the witch said in a voice of dulcet clarity, "and pity, indeed, to destroy the fine horses with which you ride the heavens. Surrender to me and you will come to no harm, neither you nor your friends. This I promise you!"

"Never!" Rothlan's answer was sharp and clear and, seeing the determination on his face, she swung swiftly out of the way, her face dark with anger.

In a ringing voice she called out in the language of the witches and, immediately, they grouped themselves in threes and fours and joined their spells together. And they aimed for the horses.

Rothlan felt Rasta jerk with a whinny of pain as the hexes hit like bolts of fire. As the pain took its breath away, the horse lost height and shrieks of pain from the other two horses told Rothlan that they had also been hit. Jaikie's horse screamed in agony and one of its wings fell useless to its side as a hex broke it. Jaikie clung to the horse in horror and Rothlan's eyes burned with rage as he watched its feeble struggles. It might make it to the ground, he thought, as it was using its remaining wing to stop it from plummeting like a stone to its death. Knowing that if the witches kept up their terrible assault, the horses would freeze in mid-air and fall to the valley floor far beneath, Rothlan called up a powerful spell; a spell that he had cast only once before. Such was the power of the jagged flash of light that streaked through the blizzard that the triumphant witches were caught by surprise and clung to their broomsticks as they were tossed in the air like feathers.

The result was immediate and dramatic. The storm carriers arrived in a deafening rumble of thunder that shook the mountains to their very roots. Lightning streaked through clouds that swirled black as the night and the witches, so long the feared mistresses of the air, looked at them in petrified wonder. The storm carriers took in the situation at a glance as they strode the heavens. Their brightly-coloured turbans framed dark, bearded faces that contorted with anger as they saw the injured horses from the stables of Ruksh screaming in pain as they struggled to stay in the sky.

Now fully aware of their danger, the snow witches turned tail and raced for safety with the storm carriers in hot pursuit. The coloured silks of their robes swirled as they swept across the heavens and their bearded faces were cruel and merciless as they reached out their great hands and crushed the witches like matchsticks.

The horses themselves called for help and one of the storm carriers, his bearded face dark with anger at the broken wings of the horses of Ruksh, swept them in his mighty arms and in an instant, his magic made them whole again.

Deep in a magic sleep, the deafening noise of the storm barely penetrated Clara's dreams but Kitor watched in trembling awe as the storm carriers, in their gaudily-coloured turbans and robes, swept the sky and wiped it clean of snow witches.

"Master," he whispered to Prince Kalman as the light of the crystal shone on him, "Lord Rothlan summoned the storm carriers and they came on the wings of the wind. Their thunder and lightning shook the mountain to its core."

"The storm carriers," muttered the prince's voice. "The witches are not powerful enough to stand against them but," he dismissed them casually, "their fate does not matter now. They captured the girl-child you spoke of and have served their purpose. But what of your captive, Kitor? Did she not try to call the storm carriers to her aid?"

"Master, she is asleep and her sleep is so deep that she barely stirred."

"Are you sure that she is the one who called out when they left Arthur's Seat?"

"I am, Master."

"Then keep her safe! As long as she is with you, I need fear nothing!"

Clara woke hours later when it was still dark. At first she didn't know where she was as even though her cloak had tried its best to cushion her from the hard ground, she was stiff, rumpled and totally disorientated. Feeling the rock of the cave beneath her, she remembered the horrors of the previous day and terror thrilled through her.

It all came back to her — the cave, Kitor the crow and the sheer drop outside that plunged the whole depth of the mountain! She froze in horror at the thought that she might have turned in her sleep and perhaps rolled towards it but, as her eyes became accustomed to the dark, she saw the round opening of the cave entrance and the stars blazing in the blackness of the heavens. The storm seemed to have passed over and the night was clear.

Dimly, she saw the shape of the crow perched on a spur of rock near the entrance to the cave. "Kitor," she whispered, "are you awake?"

Kitor woke at the sound of her voice and straightened up. A quick glance outside told him that daylight was still hours away. "It's still dark," he muttered. "Why don't you go back to sleep?"

"I've slept enough," Clara replied, "and I want to know what happened yesterday. It's stopped snowing and the sky is clear now. Where are the snow witches?"

"They have gone."

"Lord Rothlan killed them?" Clara asked hopefully.

Kitor smiled sourly. "He conjured up the storm carriers."

"The storm carriers!" said Clara, sitting up straight.

"You know them?" Kitor was impressed, despite himself.

Clara nodded. "They tried to catch me once but I was on a magic carpet and I escaped. Please, Kitor, tell me what you saw. You must have seen everything from here. What happened to the flying horses?"

"The snow witches hexed them and broke their wings. If Lord Rothlan hadn't called up the storm carriers, the witches would have finished *him* off, too."

"But he got away? Tell me, Kitor," she pleaded as he shook his head. "Please tell me! I'm your prisoner and I can't escape!"

Kitor looked at her doubtfully and shifted on his claws. His master had given him no instructions and surely there was no harm in telling her what he knew. She was a pretty child and there were tears in her eyes.

Clara saw his hestitation and smiled coaxingly. "Please, Kitor. What difference will it make?"

"The storm carriers saved the flying horses and took them away over the mountains. Tell me," he asked interestedly, "are they from the stables in Turkey called Ruksh?"

Clara nodded. "Yes, the Sultan gave us the best horses in his stables."

Kitor froze. "The Sultan! The Sultan of Turkey!" he said in a strange voice. "Sulaiman the Red? He was here? In Scotland?"

"Yes," Clara said, wishing she hadn't mentioned him.

"The Sultan of Turkey," breathed Kitor. "That explains a lot!" And he sat quite still on the spur of rock, his brain working busily as the implications of her words seethed through his mind. "He's come for his crown, hasn't he?" he said, looking at her in awe. "No wonder the prince wants you all dead!"

Clara didn't answer. She bit her lip and drew her cloak around her with trembling hands. She was sure that someone would come and save her but couldn't imagine how they would find her in this small cave in the midst of the mountains.

29. The Thunderbolt

Half-way through the morning, it started to snow again. The wind seemed to have changed direction so that the white flakes blew into the cave and layered its floor. Nothing else happened all day. Clara watched the storm and wondered why she didn't feel at all hungry. Indeed, she felt quite full. Maybe, she thought, it was part of the Sultan's magic and despite herself she was comforted. But although she told herself that someone would save her and all she really had to do was wait, she knew that while she was in the cave, she was Kalman's prisoner and at his mercy.

Kitor, meanwhile, sat like a statue on his spur of rock, waiting for another message from his master. The storm grew fiercer and he occasionally flapped his wings to get rid of the snow that continually drifted in and draped him in a white cloak. By evening, he was shivering pathetically and could barely stand on his perch.

Clara eyed him anxiously from time to time. "Kitor," she asked, "does the prince know I'm here?"

"Yes, he knows that the witches brought you. I spoke to him last night while you were asleep."

"Why did he only bring me here? Why not the others?"

"Well, the others don't matter, do they?" Kitor looked at her in surprise. "He knows that you are the one chosen to steal the crown."

"But ... how can he possibly know that?"

Kitor looked pleased with himself. "Because I was there when you left the hill and I heard you. I heard you say that you would bring back the crown!"

Relief surged through Clara. So the prince didn't know that Neil also knew the magic words! "So ... so that's why he's keeping me here?"

"As long as you are here, Clara," the crow pointed out, "the crown is safe."

Clara closed her eyes and felt real fear trickle through her. Her voice was shaky as she spoke. "Don't you know your master, Kitor?" she said urgently. "Don't you know him? The crown will only be safe when I am dead! He will leave me here to freeze or starve! Perhaps both of us!"

"The prince will not leave me here to die!" Kitor said defiantly. "I have worked well for him. He is pleased with me!" And he turned his back on her sulkily and refused to say another word.

Time dragged on until it was dark and still the wind blew and the snow fell. Clara was not cold as her cloak kept her warm but she felt very lonely and thought longingly of home and her mother.

She had, briefly, thought of attacking Kitor but had quickly given up the idea. He was the enemy, she knew, but he had wings and was her only contact with the outside world. If only she could persuade him to take a message to Lord Rothlan or Lady Ellan! Although her cloak kept her warm, she knew the bird in front of her was starving and half-frozen with the cold, yet he kept grimly to his perch and, as the day dragged miserably on, she found herself admiring him.

"Kitor," she said, as he jerked yet another layer of snow from his wings, "Kitor, why do you sit on that spur of rock? The wind blows directly over it. Come back here where it is more sheltered."

"I must stay here in case the master uses his crystal to speak to me," Kitor answered, his voice chittering with the cold.

Clara had a fair idea of how crystals worked and frowned over the crow's words. "But Kitor, he can only see us in his crystal when it's daylight. It's quite dark now. When he wants to talk to you, the light will shine and it will only take you a few seconds to perch on the rock. Surely the prince will understand?"

"Prince Kalman expects to be obeyed at all times," the crow said. "His anger is terrible even if he is disobeyed in little things."

"Oh?" Clara asked idly. The conversation helped to pass the time and Kitor had hardly spoken to her all day.

"He sends thunderbolts through the air to kill people who disobey him."

Clara hurriedly wrapped her cloak tightly round her. If Prince Kalman was in the habit of throwing thunderbolts then she devoutly hoped the magic in her cloak would protect her.

Perhaps it was the bitter cold or his growing fear that the prince might indeed leave him to die, that loosened Kitor's tongue. Clara watched apprehensively as the crow's eyes suddenly glazed with tears. They rolled down his face and froze like pearls before dropping into the snow. "Thunderbolts are terrible things! I ... I had a friend," he said sadly, "who angered him and he sent a thunderbolt to kill her. She was called Cassia and I ... well, I was fond of her."

"And still you serve him?" Clara said in a curious voice.

"He is my master and I have served him well," Kitor said stoutly, but his voice nevertheless held a trembling note of appeal. "He will not leave me to die."

"He's killing you right now," Clara snapped in exasperation. "Just look at you! You're more than half-frozen already. Kitor, don't you realize that by the morning you'll be dead?"

But the crow would not listen to her and sat stead-fastly on his spur of rock. The cold was terrible and his eyes dulled as it froze his blood.

Then, when he had all but given up hope, the light suddenly appeared, bathing him in its warm glow.

Clara saw it from the back of the cave and sat up in fear as it rested on the crow. Kitor, she saw, was now in a really dreadful state. His feathers, stiff and matted, were coated in frost and his face was pitifully thin and strained as he straightened bravely to face his master.

Kitor blinked dully as he looked into the light and, despite the crushing cold, his heart welled warm within him as he realized that his master had not, after all, forgotten him. Tears formed in his eyes and he could barely open his beak to talk. "Master!" he croaked.

"Ah, there you are, Kitor," the prince's voice was business-like. "What happened to the girl? Is she dead yet?"

Kitor's frozen face showed no change of expression. He knew perfectly well that Clara was not dead but somehow he could not bring himself to say the words that might bring a thunderbolt to kill her. Whatever happened, he knew he could not bear to see her killed like Cassia.

"She died a few hours ago, Master," his voice cracked pitifully. "The cold killed her."

There was a brief silence. "You know, you disappoint me, Kitor," the prince said dryly, "you really do. What do you take me for — a fool? I watched you in the crys-tal just a few hours ago and the girl was nowhere near dead then!"

"Master, I'm sure ..."

"I trusted you, Kitor," he said sadly, "and now ... now I find that you are lying to me. So stupid of you! I always know, you see, when people are lying to me."

Abject fear froze Kitor helplessly to his perch and
Clara watched in horror as she saw the spark of hope
fade slowly from his eyes. As he waited, numb with horror, for the thunderbolt that he was quite sure was on
its way, the prince laughed as he saw despair dawn in
the bird's eyes as it faced death.

Clara's reaction was swift, however. Grabbing a
handful of stones from the floor of the cave she flung
them at the crow and knocked him off his perch, even
as the thunderbolt shattered the spur of rock.

The beam of light found him, lying on his back with
his feet in the air, beak agape and eyes closed. And even
as she watched, tears streaming down her face, the
glow of the crystal gradually faded and left Clara alone
in the icy darkness of the cave.

She could see Kitor's body dimly illuminated by the
light of the moon and crawled towards him, ignoring
sharp jabs to her hands and knees from the broken
rock that littered the floor.

"Kitor, Kitor," she cried fearfully, "please don't be
dead!"

Kitor's beak moved and she heard a faint, pathetic
squawk as his wings fluttered weakly for an instant
and his frost-rimmed eyes blinked. The thunderbolt
had missed him by inches but he was so close to death
that he barely felt the warmth of her fingers as she
picked him up and wrapped him in the all-enveloping
comfort of her cloak.

"It's a magic cloak, Kitor," she assured him in a
whisper as she hugged him to her. "It'll keep you warm
and safe. Go to sleep now and by morning you'll be
fine."

30. Rothlan Returns

It was no more than an overhanging rock but the Ranger thought that it would give them enough protection to see them through the night. He unpacked some of the food they had been given at Inveraray but no one seemed anxious to eat; their thoughts were with Lord Rothlan, Jaikie and Hamish. Hours had passed and still there was no sign of them.

Lady Ellan gently removed Amgarad from Rihan's back. Ever since Sephia had brought him back, she had carried his frozen body under her cloak in the hope that its warmth would melt the ice that held him rigid.

Neil came up and stroked the stiff feathers with tears in his eyes. "Poor Amgarad," he said miserably. "I hope Lord Rothlan will be able to counteract the spell. I wish he'd hurry up and come back."

Lady Ellan smiled reassuringly although fear lurked in her heart. Would he ever return? She looked back to the high pass that lay between the mountains they had just crossed. All in all, they had made good speed that day for by strapping the witches' broomsticks to the sides of their horses, they had been able to see their way clearly through the snow. Neil, she knew, was tired but she had had to force the pace as long as they could hear the screams of the witches and the increasing noise of the storm.

At the time, Neil had joked about the storm carriers and hope had risen in her heart as she knew that it was possible that Rothlan had summoned them. Time passed, however, and as they flew from peak to peak and valley to valley the storm and the cries of the witches had long since faded and still Rothlan and the others had not returned. Now it was starting to get dark and they were not only hungry but the terrors of the day had left them totally exhausted.

The Ranger had just unsaddled the horses and was rubbing them down when Sephia started to whinny and prance. Lady Ellan's horse started forward with a clatter of hooves and suddenly they all galloped off down the track, their wings spreading as they took to the air.

The Ranger started to run after them and then stopped, his face suddenly wild with hope, for three horses were flying towards them with riders on their backs. "It's Lord Rothlan," he shouted, "and Hamish and Jaikie!"

The horses arrived back in a confusion of beating wings and flying hooves. Rothlan slipped from his horse and hugged Neil and Lady Ellan and shook the Ranger's hand. "Thank goodness we have found you, John. We spent ages following another trail and got hopelessly lost." He looked round sharply. "But where is Clara?" he asked.

Lady Ellan looked apprehensively at him. "Clara went to rescue Amgarad, Alasdair," she said, hating to give him bad news, "but the witches captured her."

"I see," he said. His face whitening. "Have you looked in the crystal?"

"It shows nothing," she answered. "Kalman must be hiding her from us."

His lips tightened. "And what happened to Amgarad?"

"He's here," she replied, tears stinging her eyes, "but the witches have hexed him, Alasdair, and I truly don't know whether you can bring him back to life or not."

Rothlan's face hardened. "Let me see him."

"He's over here."

They all followed her to where the great eagle lay, his wings stiffly outstretched. "I've carried him under my cloak all day," she said, "in the hope that it might warm him."

Rothlan looked suddenly weary and worried. "I wondered what had happened to Amgarad," he said. "Thank heavens Clara managed to catch him before he hit the ground!" He looked at the Ranger with a grim smile. "I'm in her debt, John!"

They stared down at the body of the eagle, its eyes glazed and its beak parted.

"Can you save him, do you think?" asked the Ranger. "Is it possible?"

Rothlan nodded. "It's possible," he said, "I only hope I've enough strength left in me to counteract the spell. My magic is nearly spent. I not only used up a lot in hexing those blasted witches out of the sky but in the end had to call up the storm carriers. They saved the horses but I didn't know that Amgarad had been hexed like this."

"If we put all the firestones together, milord," offered Hamish, "then perhaps you might be able to do it."

"Yes," agreed Jaikie, "and there are some in the saddlebags, remember? The ones the MacArthur sent with Amgarad when you were hexed by the Old Man of the Mountains."

They spread all the firestones they had over Amgarad's still body and as Lord Rothlan knelt in the snow, Lady Ellan beckoned them away so that he could concentrate on the spell.

Neil clutched his father tightly, tears running down his face as he prayed that the spell would work. Amgarad couldn't die! He just couldn't! Minutes passed and nothing happened. The Ranger and Lady Ellan looked at one another through fearful eyes. Could his spell have failed?

It was Hamish who approached Lord Rothlan and as he came closer he looked round for Amgarad, who was no longer lying stretched out on the ground, his wings stiff and straight.

"Milord?" Hamish laid a hand gently on Rothlan's shoulder and from amid the folds of his cloak, he saw Amgarad's eyes, bright and shining, looking up at him.

Hamish gave a yell of joy that brought the others at a run. "He's done it!" he shouted. "He's done it! Amgarad is alive!"

Rothlan got to his feet and stood with the eagle perched on his arm. His face was drawn and exhausted but his eyes glowed with happiness. The spell had worked and Amgarad was restored to them.

Amgarad immediately noticed that Clara was missing and it was Sephia herself who told him how they had managed to pluck him, frozen, from the skies.

"Clara wasn't hurt," she assured the eagle. "The witches took her. They knocked her off my back and caught her on their broomsticks."

"Take heart, Ranger, we'll get her back," Lady Ellan said, seeing the pain on his face. "I know things look black but believe me, she will take no harm. The Sultan's spell will protect her."

They ate well that evening on the remainder of the cold meat, oatcakes and cheese that the Campbells had given them. Indeed, Archie Campbell had pressed more on them than he could afford to give, such was his gratitude — for before they'd left Inveraray, Rothlan had magnificently repaid the Campbell chief for his hospitality. Noticing signs of want in the gaunt faces of the clansmen, he had cast a spell that lifted the blight that was affecting their cattle and, although Archie Campbell did not realize it at the time, his fortunes and those of his clan were to grow and prosper from that day forth.

Amgarad, too, fed well on an unsuspecting rabbit that had fallen victim to his claws and then spent the rest of the evening meticulously cleaning his feathers. Tomorrow, they would have to serve him well, for, like the others, he worried about Clara and planned to spend the day scouring the mountains for her.

In Edinburgh, Mrs MacLean was also worrying about her daughter. She'd been fast asleep when a picture of Clara had crept into her unconscious mind. Clara, lying in a cold, dark cave. Turning and tossing restlessly as the nightmare took hold, she cried out in her sleep but it was only when a brilliant flash of light streaked across her dream that she woke with a start and sat up in bed. After that, she hadn't been able to settle and morning saw her heavy-eyed and consumed with worry.

"I just *know* something's wrong with Clara," she said aloud as she poured boiling water from the kettle into the teapot and carried it to the kitchen table. "Neil's all right. Somehow I'm quite sure of that. But Clara's definitely in trouble. I'm her mother, and mothers always know!"

As the tea brewed, she sat clutching and unclutching the firestone that Lady Ellan had given her. I must try to get hold of Sir James, she thought, looking at the clock. He'll know what to do. But after breakfast, when she called Sir James, his housekeeper told her that he was away from home and even his mobile number was unobtainable.

She sighed. She could tell she was in a state from the way she was walking up and down the kitchen, twisting the tea towel in her hands. You know what you have to do, Janet, she told herself firmly. You just don't have the courage, that's what it is. And again she picked up the firestone that Lady Ellan had given her and saw the strange, sparkling dragonfire in its depths. But I've got to do something! Clara's in trouble! I just know it!

She stared round the kitchen, totally ordinary and familiar and as far removed from magic as one could possibly imagine. And yet, she thought, here she was with a magic stone in her hand — a magic stone that could call up a magic carpet that would take her to Clara . . .

"Get a grip, Janet," she said aloud. "You know you've got to call your carpet."

With that, she went into the hall where she put on her coat and tied a scarf round her head. Placing the firestone carefully in a pocket of her handbag, she went into the garden, locked the door of the house behind her and standing on the garden path, took a deep breath. "Carpet," she said firmly, and clapped her hands.

31. Arthur Casts a Spell

While Clara sat huddled, fearful and lonely, in the cave in the mountains and Mrs MacLean tossed and turned in the throes of her nightmare, other important events were happening in the world of magic; for the MacArthur had been busy and was now putting his cunning plan into action.

They were all there on the slopes of Arthur's Seat: Sir James, Tatler and the Chief Constable, as well as a whole host of MacArthurs who had come to wish Archie and Arthur a safe journey. Standing on a crag, high up on the hill, Sir James, like the others, was bitterly cold and, stamping his feet to keep his circulation going, drew his winter coat closer around him. Despite its thickness, it was poor protection against a wind that was steadily freezing him to the marrow and, despite his excitement, he thought longingly of hot baths and central heating; for the slopes of Arthur's Seat at two o'clock in the morning had little to offer in the way of comfort.

As they stood there, huddled against the biting wind, the MacArthur, Tatler, Sir James and the Chief Constable all peered at their watches from time to time and, as the hour approached, Sir James started the countdown. "Ten, nine, eight, seven, six, five, four, three, two, one, zero ..." he muttered.

When he reached "zero," they all looked up expectantly, casting their eyes over the vast stretch of lights that glittered, spider-like, over Edinburgh and beyond and, exactly as planned, each and every light went out. Emergency generators suddenly cranked into life all over the city, electrical engineers swore as they were dragged out of bed to attend to the emergency and those hapless individuals caught in the dark, were reduced to feeling their way home without even the comforting gleam of moonlight to help them on their way. It was a moonless night, which was exactly why the MacArthur had chosen it!

Sir James switched on his torch, as did the others, and turned to look at the side of the hill where Archie and Arthur were waiting.

He was a magnificent dragon, thought Sir James, as he watched Arthur move out of the tunnel, clawing his way awkwardly towards them. Curls of smoke blew from his nostrils as he flapped his wings, delighted at being above ground again.

Archie, dressed in sheepskin from top to toe, made his way over to them, guided by the light of their torches.

"You look a bit like an Eskimo in all that gear," Sir James laughed, pulling at the fur-lined hood that framed his face.

"Aye," Archie grinned, "but on a night like this, I'll need every bit of it. And it'll be colder still once I'm out over the sea."

"You're quite sure you know what you've to do then?" checked the MacArthur.

Archie nodded and indicated the saddlebags that hung over Arthur's back. "It's all there," he nodded. "Don't worry, we'll be fine. Arthur's looking forward to the fun of it all and," he said looking around, "as it's a dark night, I doubt if anybody out there'll spot us!"

"Watch out for the oil rigs, though," Tatler cautioned. "They have their own power supply and they'll be as brightly lit as Christmas trees."

"I'll mind out for them," Archie grinned, climbing onto Arthur's back and gripping the saddle as he settled himself comfortably.

Arthur listened carefully as the MacArthur spoke to him seriously and nodded his great head understandingly. "Remember, Arthur, their radar can't pick you up. Just avoid the ships' lights and you ought to be okay."

The MacArthur then stepped back and they all waved to Archie as Arthur's wings started to sweep through the air with increasing strength.

"Good luck," Sir James called as they watched the great dragon soar effortlessly upwards, his massive bulk swallowed immediately by the darkness of the night sky.

"How long," asked the Chief Constable, looking after him in wonder, "do you think it'll take him?"

"The best part of the night, I should think," answered the MacArthur. "He has quite a way to travel, you know — although, of course, a lot depends on where the French fleet is lying!"

Archie was well-nigh frozen stiff by the time the French fleet came into view. Although he'd been alert and excited as they'd soared over the invisible mass of the darkened coastline, the monotony of flying over the dark waters of the North Sea soon palled as an occupation; especially as the night was pitch black and he couldn't see anything at all.

Arthur, however, being a dragon, didn't suffer from this disadvantage, for his wonderful eyes could see equally well in both the dark and the daylight. Flying directly out to sea, he gave a couple of brilliantly lit oil rigs a wide berth, avoided a few helicopters and then, veering southwards, curved towards the fish-rich waters of the Dogger Bank where he was pretty sure he would find the French trawlers and their accompanying naval escort.

Archie's first indication that they were approaching the French fleet was the sudden gleam and twinkle of lights from a myriad of fishing boats, and a more stately glow from vessels that were obviously much bigger.

"There they are, Arthur! It must be the French! Gosh, there are loads of boats!" Archie said excitedly.

"Let's check," Arthur said, losing height rapidly until he literally swooped over the waves so that Archie could read the names on the sides of the trawlers.

"Marie Claire," Archie read one of the names aloud, "Cherbourg." His brow creased. "Cherbourg," he repeated. "That's a French port! It's them, all right! Come on, Arthur, let's get started!"

As Arthur flew over the fishing fleet, Archie loosened the saddlebags so that a constant stream of glittering magic dust floated through the air and landed in and around the trawlers and although some of the fishermen, scanning the surrounding blackness fearfully, seemed to sense the presence of something unusual, there was no sudden outcry to indicate that he had been spotted.

The battleships, however, proved quite a different kettle of fish for, as Arthur and his magic dust swept across the French fleet in the total, utter darkness of the night, he was spotted! Not by the glow of the ships' lights, for he was too high for that, but by the wonders of modern technology.

It was the MacArthur's fault, really. Not quite up to scratch with the latest in military inventions, he had omitted to include night-vision goggles in his calculations. Indeed, he'd never heard of them and had relied on the fact that Arthur didn't show up on radar screens to afford him protection.

This, however, wasn't enough and before long one of the officers on watch caught sight of his great shape flying over the biggest and most illustrious of all the French battleships.

At first, needless to say, he just couldn't believe his eyes. He took his goggles off, polished them up with his handkerchief and eyed the battleship again. By that time, however, Arthur had moved on and there was nothing to see. He sighed with relief but now on the alert, started to scan the sky above the nearby ships. And he spotted Arthur again.

"Hey, Henri," he called, beckoning another officer onto the bridge. "Come here a minute, will you."

"What's up, Jacques?"

"Put your goggles on and look over there," Jacques said, hurriedly. "Hurry up, put them on and tell me what you see. Over there ... to starboard. What the devil's that?"

"It looks," Henri said, his eyes round in disbelief as he adjusted the night vision, "it looks a bit like a dragon, wouldn't you say?"

"That's what I thought!" They looked at one another apprehensively.

"The radar room," Jacques said sharply as reality kicked in. "What in heaven's name are they doing down there? They should have spotted it ages ago. It should never have got within a mile of us!" He swore roundly as they left the bridge at a gallop and charged down the companionway. "Why the devil haven't they sounded the alarm!"

The sailors manning the quietly-bleeping banks of radar screens looked up in surprise as the two officers barged hurriedly into the room and made straight for the monitors, peering at them over the men's shoulders.

"Hey," one of them protested. "what's all this?"

Henri couldn't believe his eyes. "They're . . . they're not picking anything up, Jacques," he said incredulously, ignoring the question and peering at the screen over the operator's shoulder. "Not a thing!"

"Maybe if you were to tell me what I should be picking up, sir, it might help?" queried the radar operator dryly.

Henri and Jacques looked at one another.

Jacques took a deep breath. "There's something huge flying over the fleet," he said. "I don't know what it is but it looks like an enormous dragon!"

The radar operators looked at one another and grinned. "You *are* having us on, sir, aren't you?"

"No, I'm not! We both saw it."

Henri nodded. "Whatever it is, it's cruising over the fleet right now!"

The radar operators glanced at their screens, just to check, and, seeing nothing, looked at their officers through narrowed eyes. There was nothing there and they were not impressed.

"I wonder if they're going to wake the captain up," said one wickedly, glancing at his friends for support. "Although I can't say *I'd* like to wake up the old man with a tale like that!"

There was burst of laughter as Jacques and Henri looked at one another in disgust and left them to the green glow of their radar screens. Scrambling up the companionway to the bridge, they hastily pulled on their goggles and once more scanned the darkness of the heavens.

This time, however, the sky was completely and utterly empty. They looked at one another in dismay — for the monstrous creature that they had seen soaring in the blackness of the night sky had completely vanished.

Frantically, they scanned the surrounding area again and again but there was no dragon to be seen anywhere and it was just when they had decided that it must have been a figment of their imagination that one of the radio officers came up to them and handed them a piece of paper. Jacques scanned it quickly and looked at Henri in triumph. "It wasn't only us that spotted it," he burst out, thrusting the paper into his hands. "Look at this! An officer on one of the cruisers saw it too!"

"But where has it gone?" Henri questioned, looking up in to the darkness. "It seems to have completely disappeared."

By then, they were far too late to catch a glimpse of Arthur for he had finished his work and, with Archie perched tiredly on his back, was was already heading for home.

32. Scotch Mist

Sir James, Tatler and the Chief Constable all spent the night inside the hill. Sir James had become used to the wide, stone-flagged corridors that arched dimly towards the sleeping quarters, but Tatler and the Chief Constable marvelled at the size of rooms that housed vast wardrobes and huge four-poster beds. Tapestries, depicting dragons, unicorns and other strange creatures, draped the walls, and the old furniture gleamed with polished brilliance. Sir James relaxed for a while in the welcome warmth of a fire that burned brightly in the depth of an enormous fireplace and then, totally exhausted, headed for bed. As he pulled the blankets and fur covers over him, he had only time to think momentarily of Arthur and Archie, flying over the icy waves of the North Sea, before his eyes closed and sleep overtook him.

They all slept late and it was almost ten o'clock when they gathered for breakfast in the Great Hall where Hamish told them that Archie and Arthur had returned safely just before dawn.

"It all went without a hitch," the MacArthur assured them in a voice filled with satisfaction as they poured themselves coffee.

"Wonderful," Sir James congratulated him.

"When will you know if the spell has worked?" Tatler asked, a trifle anxiously. "I thought I'd better check before I passed the news on to Charles Wyndham and the Prime Minister."

"It's working already," the MacArthur grinned gleefully. "Archie and Arthur have just gone to get cleaned up. They'll be back in a minute but we had a look in the crystal when they came in, and from the way the French are behaving it seems to have just dawned on them that they're in big trouble!"

They strolled over to the stand that held the crystal and stared into its depth. As it showed nothing more than a thick, white mist it was hardly exciting viewing but Sir James sighed with relief. The MacArthur's cunning plan was working a treat!

"The spell will take care of the French," nodded the MacArthur, looking round the table, "but it's the crown that's our main concern now." His voice became serious as they sat back and listened. "I spoke to Ellan earlier on and she told me that Rothlan, Hamish and Jaikie have finally managed to rejoin them. I told you that Kalman set the snow witches onto them, didn't I? Rothlan had to call up the storm carriers to finish them off but he lost Clara and Amgarad in the battle. Amgarad was frozen by the witches' spells but apparently he's fine now."

"And Clara?" Sir James asked anxiously as Tatler and the Chief Constable looked at one another in alarm.

The MacArthur frowned. "Kalman is using the crown's magic to hide her from us. The crystals haven't been able to pick her up at all."

"But that's dreadful." Sir James looked horrified.

"Don't worry, Sir James," the MacArthur reassured him. "You're forgetting the Sultan's spell. Kalman might be able to keep her prisoner but he won't be able to harm her. He'd know immediately that a strong spell is protecting her."

"Aren't Lord Rothlan and her father trying to find her?" queried the Chief Constable.

"Amgarad is going to search the mountains for her today, but the others have to press on to Ardray."

"Did you tell Rothlan about Kalman's meeting with the Scottish Executive tomorrow?" queried Sir James.

"I did. At three o'clock, you said."

Sir James nodded. "It's *so* important that Rothlan moves into the tower at the right time," he said, frowning worriedly. "I'm getting totally paranoid about it!"

The MacArthur nodded. "So am I," he admitted. "Time's getting short. They just *have* to find Clara soon. Rothlan can't change back to the twenty-first century until they do."

Sir James looked worried. "I hope to goodness our plan works," he muttered. "Kalman seems to have been winning all along the line. What if he cancels this meeting?"

"Relax, James. He can't afford to miss it. You know that," the MacArthur said seriously. "Not if it's going to prove his claim beyond doubt!"

Sir James frowned as he looked round the table. "Parliament is absolutely buzzing with it all," he said to Tatler and Sir Archie, "and to tell you the truth I find it totally mind-boggling the way everybody is supporting his claim. Believe me; I haven't dared say a word against him! They're for him to a man, just as he planned." He heaved a sigh and shook his head.

"Then there's no doubt that he'll be proclaimed king?" Tatler said.

"No doubt at all! The latest news is that de Charillon's waiting for a courier who's bringing more papers from Paris. If they arrive in time, he'll pass them on to Stuart and, according to Ned, they'll provide absolute proof."

The MacArthur drank the remains of his coffee. "Aye, that I can well believe," he said sourly. "Forgeries, the lot of them!"

They all rose to their feet as Arthur and Archie appeared. Sir James slapped Archie on the back with a beaming smile and there were murmurs of congratulation all round. Arthur perched happily beside the MacArthur and was about to join in the conversation when he glimpsed the glow of the crystal ball.

"Did you know that the mist's vanished?" he queried.

The MacArthur got up and adjusted the crystal. "It's all right," he said reassuringly as they all sprang to their feet in alarm, "it's just homed in on something else." His face creased in a puzzled frown. "Where do you think *this* is?" he asked.

Tatler looked over his shoulder and almost had a heart attack as he looked at the figures that moved in the crystal. "That's Bruiton!" he gasped. "The French Foreign Minister! I don't know where he is but it's him all right!"

With one accord they clustered round the crystal and watched with fascinated eyes as Marcel Bruiton, followed by a horde of officials, marched into what looked like a vast, underground room.

"It must be part of the Ministry of Defence in Paris," Tatler muttered as he eyed the uniformed figures.

"In that case, this ought to prove very interesting," the Chief Constable said, with a grin as they settled excitedly to watch the French reaction to the MacArthur's cunning plan.

33. French Leave

Tatler was correct in his guess. What they were seeing was, indeed, an operations room in the Ministry of Defence in Paris. The eye of the crystal moved round it slowly, revealing a huge, brightly-coloured projection that dominated one of the walls. It showed, in great detail, the blue stretch of the North Sea from the east coast of Great Britain to the deeply indented coastline of Norway. A casual observer might have assumed that a giant computer game was in progress as the map was dotted with a variety of ships of varying sizes that were either strung along the shores of Britain or clustered in the middle of the screen. Those in the middle of the sea, it was noted, were flying little French flags.

Army, Navy and Air Force uniforms were all present in the room but it was the naval officers, stationed nearest the screen, whose faces showed traces of strain. The Army and Air Force officers seemed decidedly more relaxed and clung interestedly to the outer fringes of the group, their expressions guarded. Nevertheless, one could, if one looked closely, occasionally discern a fleeting look of amusement on their carefully schooled features. The navy was in the soup! Or rather, in the middle of the North Sea without a lifebelt in sight!

"Well?" Bruiton demanded.

"It's quite incredible!" answered the most senior of his admirals, shaking his head worriedly. "Nothing's changed! I just don't know what the devil's going on out there. Apparently, the fleet is surrounded by a heavy, thick, white mist. It sits out there covering our entire fleet and, as far as I can see, defies all the laws of meteorology!"

"And can't," Marcel Bruiton demanded, "can't they sail through it?"

The admiral gave him an expressionless look. "They've been trying to sail through it all day, Minister."

"What! You must be joking!"

"I'm not," the admiral muttered.

"But ... I don't understand ..."

"Neither do I," muttered the admiral, "and what's more, neither does the Weather Bureau. Not only that, the satellite shows that the fleet is sailing round in circles."

"Round in circles!" snapped Bruiton. "You'd think with all the expensive navigational equipment we've installed that they'd be able to do slightly better than that!"

"Our captains at sea blame everyone but themselves, sir."

"Don't be ridiculous! Anyway, surely they can't *all* be going round in circles!"

"Fantastic or not, that's what they're doing!" the admiral paused. "All of them."

"Even ... even the submarines?" gulped the Minister.

"Even the submarines!"

"And what about the British fleet? What are they doing? Where," his eyes searched the board, "where are they?"

"Laughing their heads off, I should think!" whispered a high-ranking officer to his neighbour.

The admiral blenched. "Sir, they're doing nothing." He gestured to the screen where ships bearing the white ensign of the British Navy hugged the coast.

"Their entire fleet is in port. They haven't a warship or a submarine at sea!"

"But they must know that our fleet is on its way to destroy them?"

Several heads jerked in surprise at this remark. "*Destroy* them?" queried a rather crusty-looking old general, looking round a room that had fallen suddenly silent. "Is there, by any chance, something that we haven't been told, Minister? I, certainly, was under the impression that the cause of our present state of alert was the protection of our fishing fleet!"

"Yes, yes," Bruiton said hastily, "a slip of the tongue! I meant destroy them ... if they attacked our fleet."

The general coughed. "May I point out, Minister," he said, "that the entire British fleet is in port and that at the moment we seem to have put ourselves in the position of aggressors! Besides which," he glowered at the admiral, "our fleet must be in a disgraceful state of unreadiness if all it can do is sail round in circles. Thick mist or no thick mist!"

Biting back an angry retort, the Minister looked thoughtful. "The mist is suspicious," he announced.

"Very suspicious," nodded the admiral, pleased that they were in agreement about something.

"Can't we have it analysed?"

"We could analyse it, sir," there was an agonised pause, "if we were able to find it."

"But," he looked at the admiral, "you've just said it was around our fleet!"

"Yes, it is, sir. We have proof of that. Our captains confirm it."

"Then why can't it be analysed? Am I surrounded by fools?"

"Well, you see, Minister, there are no chemists on board the warships."

"But for God's sake, man, the Weather Bureau can send in an aircraft equipped to take samples, surely!"

"Theoretically, yes," agreed the admiral, swallowing hard.

There was a stunned silence as the Minister digested this reply. "What the devil do you mean?" he said eventually. "Theoretically, yes!"

The admiral didn't answer and as the uneasy silence lengthened, an Air Force officer moved over and saluted respectfully. "We've been sending weather aircraft out to take samples, sir. They've flown out to the areas indicated but they haven't found the mist." He took a deep breath and his eyes shifted to a point over the minister's left shoulder, "and what's more important, sir, neither have they found the fleet."

This time the silence lasted for several minutes.

Incredulity laced the Minister's voice. *"They – can't – find – the – fleet!"*

"No, sir."

"What on earth do you mean," his voice was strangled, "they can't find the fleet?"

The admiral looked as though he were about to burst into tears. "It ... it seems to be lost!"

"Lost! What do you mean it's lost? Good heavens, man, you can't just *lose* the French fleet!"

"Sir," interrupted the Air Force officer, "when the weather aircraft returned and the crew reported that they were unable to find either the fog or the fleet we sent over one of our best reconnaissance aircraft."

"Well?"

"With exactly the same results, sir. The weather, as far as they are concerned, is as clear as crystal from Norway to Scotland and our fleet is non-existent."

"It's not there? But where can it have gone?"

"No, no. You don't understand, sir," interrupted the admiral, "it's there, all right. Our commanders and captains are sending in reports regularly!"

"So, it's there — and it's not there! There's a mist — and there isn't a mist! Is that what you're trying to tell me?"

"Yes, sir," whispered the unhappy admiral, staring at his feet.

The Minister, ageing ten years in as many seconds, looked as though he was going to have a nervous breakdown on the spot. "A secret weapon! It must be!" he said glancing round the room sharply. "The British must have a secret weapon! There ... there can be no other explanation."

"What are your orders, sir? What shall we do?"

"Call the fleet back immediately!" he snarled. "I've a strong suspicion that you'll find that the mist will lift the minute it heads for France!"

"And the fishing boats, sir?"

"No, leave them. We'll continue to monitor them by satellite. It will be interesting to see if anything happens to *them.*"

With that, he stalked out of the room and, with his departure, the crystal started to cloud over.

Tatler looked absolutely rapturous. "We've won! We've won!" he said, throwing his arms in the air and dancing round like a madman. "He's withdrawn the fleet! MacArthur, you're fantastic! I only hope Wyndham and the PM were watching on their crystal! The PM will be over the moon, believe me! Absolutely over the moon!"

34. The Reluctant Broomstick

Amgarad flew high, his sharp eyes scanning the craggy peaks of the mountains that lay stretched below him like a black and white carpet; for in the valleys, the snow lay thick and deep.

The air was crisp and clear, however, and as he quartered the slopes below, his heart sank at the immensity of the task he had set himself. The snow witches, he knew, could have taken Clara anywhere. And even if she were in the open, her magic cloak would make it virtually impossible for him to see her.

Hours passed as he methodically searched the multitude of mountains and valleys that seemed to stretch endlessly beneath him and, as the day wore on and night started to fall, was actually thinking of returning to his master when a movement far beneath him, caught his eye. As he snapped his wings back and swooped lower, a gleam of amusement spread across his face. This was certainly something to save to tell Archie and Arthur when he got back to the hill!

Far below him, a large, black crow was attempting to ride a broomstick and making a complete hash of it; for the broomstick was diving, swooping and looping-the-loop in its efforts to rid itself of its unwelcome passenger. The crow, to give it its due, seemed equally determined to stay on and as it flapped wildly in an effort to keep its balance — not exactly easy when upside down — Amgarad remembered the crow that had followed them from Edinburgh. His eyes sharpened and his dive steepened.

Between trying to keep his balance and thinking of how pleased Clara was going to be when he brought her the broomstick, Kitor was much too occupied to think of danger and for once neglected to observe the first rule of the wild. Watch your back, always, all the time!

It wasn't surprising, therefore, that he almost had a heart attack when Amgarad swooped, caught the broomstick in his talons and eyed him grimly. Wings flapping frantically, Kitor held on as the broomstick steadied and then gulped fearfully at the sight of the great eagle whose beak was mere inches from his face. To avoid certain death, he knew what he had to say — and he said it fast.

"Clara," he gabbled, "I know where she is! I can take you to her."

Amgarad tightened his grip on the broomstick with such ferocity that he almost cracked the wood. The broomstick shrieked in pain and Kitor nearly fell off at the sudden noise.

"Where is she?" Amgarad said. "Tell me at once!"

"I'll do better than that; I'll take you to her. It isn't far now. Look, you can see it. That cave in the side of the mountain over there."

"Why the broomstick?" Amgarad's eyes were fierce.

"Well, she can't fly, can she?" answered Kitor, relief making him chatty. "We talked about it this morning and she reckoned that some of the witches' broomsticks might still be lying round after the battle. She thought she might be able to fly one, but to be honest, I don't know if she will. I haven't been able to get this one to fly in a straight line all morning!"

Amgarad looked ahead to the small dark opening in the side of the mountain and his heart lifted as he saw Clara standing at the entrance to the cave, waving to him.

"Amgarad!" he heard her voice faintly on the wind. "Am-garad!"

It took only a few minutes for Amgarad to reach the cave. Clara jumped up and down in excitement as he swooped in with Kitor clinging frantically to the broomstick as it brushed the walls of the cave.

"Amgarad!" she cried. "Thank goodness you're not frozen any more! I *knew* that Lord Rothlan could undo the witches' spell! Oh, it's wonderful to see you again!" And seeing Kitor sitting rather dejectedly on the broomstick, she knelt down so that he could hop onto her arm. "I'm glad to see you too, Kitor," she smiled, straightening up. "You've been gone for ages but thank you for finding me a broomstick!"

"Kitor!" Amgarad's eyes grew suddenly stern. "Prince Kalman has a crow called Kitor! Is the prince not your master, crow?"

Kitor looked at Clara and shifted on his claws, too petrified to speak.

"Kitor saved my life, Amgarad," Clara said swiftly, coming to his aid. "He told the prince that I was dead when I wasn't but somehow the prince knew he was lying. He sent a thunderbolt to kill him but I managed to save him." She looked from Kitor to Amgarad. "He is one of us now, Amgarad," she smiled, looking at him anxiously, for he was not normally quite so fierce-looking. "He was bringing the broomstick for me — so that I could escape from this awful cave."

Amgarad looked at the crow who met his eyes steadily.

"If your master, Lord Rothlan, will have me," Kitor said, "I will be proud to serve him."

"You can ask him yourself, Kitor," Amgarad replied, "for we are going to him now." He looked disparagingly at the broomstick. "Once I've sorted out this broomstick, that is!"

He gripped the broomstick in his claws and spoke to
it with deceptive gentleness. "You are going to carry
this girl, broomstick, and carry her safely. I want none
of your tricks, do you understand?"

The broomstick, who had already felt the power of
Amgarad's claws, hastened to agree and, as a sign of its
good intentions, immediately floated into the air and
hovered steadily beside them.

"No tricks, mind," Amgarad warned, "or I'll turn
you into matchwood!"

The broomstick trembled at the very thought. "You're
scaring it, Amgarad," Clara chided as she climbed on.
"I'm sure it will behave beautifully."

Amgarad looked at her sideways. "It had better," he
said. "Don't forget that it was once a witch's broomstick!" He turned to the crow. "Kitor, will you fly alongside Clara? Just to make sure the broomstick behaves
itself. I'll lead the way over the mountains."

Amgarad launched himself into space and Kitor
flapped beside her as the broomstick flew out over the
precipice that dropped from the cave entrance. Clara,
who still didn't like heights, kept her eyes firmly shut
as she sailed out of the cave on the broomstick. Even
when they had left the mountain behind and she judged
it safe to open her eyes, she felt decidedly uneasy at
being so high. Broomsticks, after all, were thin things
compared to the solid safety of Sephia's broad back!

The journey, fortunately, was not long and as they
started to glide downwards she could see the distant
gleam of the sea.

"Look, Clara," said Kitor, "look over to your left. Can
you see the forest and the Black Tower? That is Ardray,
the home of Prince Kalman!"

"Ardray!" she repeated, startled, for she hadn't realized that they were that close. She paled and gripped

the broomstick tightly as she turned her head — and as she looked she gasped in wonder for nothing had prepared her for the sight of Prince Kalman's grimly beautiful castle.

Until then she hadn't really given much thought to its appearance and the soaring majestic grandeur of the vision that met her eyes was totally unexpected. It took her breath away completely. This, she thought, was a magician's castle if ever there was one. She stared at it, round-eyed and totally entranced. Tall and turreted, with carved, winged eagles decorating its balconies, the Black Tower of Ardray reared high, proud and elegant above the trees of the magic forest.

35. Kitor Joins the Club

Even as Clara looked towards the Black Tower fascinated by its magnificent grandeur, she heard a distant shout and peering downwards, saw a group of riders looking up at her from the snow-covered hillside.

"Clara!" her father's voice mirrored his relief as he saw her on the broomstick.

"*Serai!*" ordered Lord Rothlan. And the black horses of Ruksh grew their wings and soared into the air to meet them.

Clara laughed in delight as the great horses soared round her. Neil and Lady Ellan flew alongside her as the broomstick gradually lost height and, once they landed, her father caught her in his arms and swung her round and round in the air.

"Clara," he said, "thank goodness you're back. I was worried out of my mind the whole time you were away!"

"I'm glad to be back, too," she said, her eyes full of tears as everyone made a fuss of her. "I was frightened at first but after a while I knew I would come to no harm. The Sultan's spell and the magic cloak protected me."

Rothlan looked at Clara with relief. "Thank goodness you're safe, Clara," he said. "Now that we're all together again, I can, at last, hex us back into the twenty-first century." And with that, he left the group and strode forward to stand on a great spur of rock that jutted out over the stream. As Neil, Jaikie and Hamish watched the cloaked figure in fascination, they heard him recite the words of a spell. As he stood with his arms spread out to the gathering gloom, there was a sudden, breathless hush as though the world stood still. The air seemed to ripple alarmingly round them and the mountains wavered unsteadily for a few seconds and then settled. They looked at him questioningly as he returned and he smiled at their anxious faces.

"Relax," he said, "I've just taken us back into the twenty-first century!"

Neil looked round, slightly stunned. "But ... nothing's changed," he said. "Everything's still the same."

"Well, I don't suppose mountains change that much over the centuries," Jaikie said, "but if you look over there," he pointed along the glen, "you can see the lights of cars on a road."

Relief flooded through Neil in comforting waves. The familiar sight of headlights and telegraph poles made him realize just how much he appreciated being back in his own time.

"What about Ardray?" he asked Jaikie, looking over the glen to the silver glint of the sea. "Is *it* still there?"

"It's still there, don't worry," grinned Jaikie. "You'll be able to see it because you're wearing a firestone but it will be invisible to the ordinary people who live round about."

Rothlan strode over to them. "I think we should rest here," he said, meeting the Ranger's eyes for, despite Clara's assurances, she looked tired and drawn.

Amgarad coughed and meeting Lord Rothlan's eyes, nodded towards the crow, who sat somewhat apprehensively beside him.

Rothlan turned to the bird and held out his arm so that Kitor could perch on it. Kitor fluttered up and looked anxiously into brown eyes that were very different from the cold, blue eyes of Prince Kalman.

"Lord Rothlan," Clara said anxiously. "Kitor saved my life, really he did! He didn't want the prince to send a thunderbolt to kill me so he told him a lie. *And* he was trying to bring me a broomstick so that I could get out of that dreadful cave. He could have just flown away and left me, but he didn't."

"You have a good friend in Clara," Rothlan said, smiling slightly and looking at Kitor appraisingly. "Well, crow, do you renounce your allegiance to Prince Kalman?"

Kitor nodded emphatically. "Yes, master," he said.

"Will you serve me, Kitor? Faithfully, unto death?"

"I will, master," the crow said proudly, "faithfully, unto death!"

Rothlan smiled. "Then I bid you welcome to my service," he said, passing his hand over the crow in a protective gesture. "In fact, you have already served me, Kitor, and you have my thanks — indeed, you have everyone's thanks — for rescuing Clara, who is dear to us all." There was a murmur of agreement and even the Ranger, who had no great opinion of crows in general, spoke kindly to him and placed him on his shoulder.

There was a bustle of activity as they set up camp by the tumbling, mountain stream and although Clara had her first proper meal in days she ate very little and, as Neil watched her anxiously, fell into an exhausted sleep. Kitor, however, ate well; for Amgarad had gone hunting and invited him to share his kill.

"Tell us about Ardray, Kitor," invited Lord Rothlan, once they had all finished eating. "We are near the edge of the forest now and over the years I've heard many strange tales about it — and the evil things that live in it."

Kitor shivered. "Indeed, master, it is a frightening place to pass through and dangerous even to those who fly over it, for although you and your horses will be able to cross it freely, it can still destroy you."

"What would happen to us?" asked Neil interestedly.

Kitor shifted uneasily on his claws and lowered his voice as they leant forward to listen to his words. "The trees in its forest are magic trees," he said. "The undersides of their leaves are crusted white with a drug that makes you lose your memory. The great red balls that hang from them are not flowers. They are tightly-curled balls of creepers that catch strangers in their coils. If you fly high, you can avoid the creepers but the leaves would release their poison into the air and you and the horses would forget everything — even why you were there at all."

Lady Ellan shuddered. "How horrible," she said, looking in alarm at the crow. "What else is there?"

"Goblins," answered Kitor, "evil creatures that live in the darkness under the roots of the trees. I've never seen them myself but I've heard tell of them. They keep watch from inside hollow trees and move the paths here and there so that strangers get lost and can never find their way out. It is said that no one can reach the Black Tower of Ardray while the goblins are on guard."

"If what you say is true then perhaps it might be better to use broomsticks to get to the tower instead of the horses," Rothlan said thoughtfully.

Kitor put his head to one side. "You're right, master," he said approvingly, "broomsticks would be much better. Why, with them you could fly straight into the room of mirrors. The prince wouldn't keep the crown anywhere else."

"That means that one of you would have to stay behind to look after the horses," Rothlan said, glancing across at Jaikie and Hamish. "They're far too valuable to leave unattended."

"Won't the prince be watching us in his crystal, though?" asked Neil, looking round apprehensively. "Now that we're back in the twenty-first century, he could be looking at us at this very minute! After all, he must know that we're close to Ardray. Surely he'll be keeping an eye on us?"

"It's getting dark, Neil. If he tried to see us just now, the light from the crystal would give him away."

"But if we get too close to the crown, he could just walk into the tower through his mirror and take it back to Edinburgh! What'll we do if he does that and it isn't in the tower when we get inside?"

"We thought about that when we made our plans, Neil, and we've taken it into consideration. You see, the crown is only really safe when it is in the tower; there's no way he would ever leave it unattended in the Edinburgh house. We're going to strike at a time when he can't look in his crystal or walk through his mirrors; a time when he's out of his house and with other people. As he will be when he has his meeting in parliament tomorrow afternoon."

"Anyway," added Kitor, "he must be feeling quite safe at the moment. He knows that Clara was chosen to steal the crown and he thinks she's still trapped in the cave."

"Clara! Chosen to steal the crown? Why would he think that?" queried the Ranger.

"Because," said Kitor taking a trembling breath, "because I told him so. I heard Clara calling to her mother when she left Arthur's Seat. She said she would bring back the crown. I'm ... I'm truly sorry," he stammered.

Amgarad clicked his beak fiercely but Rothlan's face was calm as he looked at the bird thoughtfully. "That is in the past, Kitor and it is forgiven," he said with a wry smile, "but you actually misled the prince, you know, for Neil also knows the magic words that will restore the crown to us."

"John! John, can you hear me?"

They swung round as the voice spoke out of the air just beside them. Neil looked at his father in amazement and they both jumped to their feet.

"Mum?" Neil said anxiously, looking round.

"Where are you, Janet?" the Ranger said.

"I'm here, on this carpet," the voice said. "Just a minute." Mrs. MacLean wriggled to the side of her carpet, swung her legs over the edge and appeared before them.

"Mum? What on earth are you doing here?"

"It's Clara," she said. "I had to come. I was worried about Clara, so I called the carpet and came." She looked round and her voice rose in alarm as she realized that Clara wasn't there. "Where is she? Why isn't she here?"

"Calm down, Janet," her husband said, looking at Neil and Lord Rothlan in alarm. "Clara's all right."

Lady Ellan smiled and, moving over to Mrs MacLean, kissed her on both cheeks. "Janet," she said softly, "how very nice to see you. Now, don't worry. Clara's asleep just now but if you take your coat off and sit down, I'll wake her up."

"Never mind my coat, I must see her. I'll come with you."

Lady Ellan led her over to where Clara lay, sound asleep.

"She looks ill," her mother said, leaning over and looking at her closely. "She's been ill, hasn't she?"

Lady Ellan looked helplessly at the Ranger. She didn't want to panic Janet by telling her Clara had been caught by snow witches.

"We got separated, Mum," Neil said, pulling at his mother's arm so that she listened to him. "Clara ended up stuck in a cave for a couple of days but her cloak kept her warm and Kitor, here," he indicated the crow, "Kitor looked after her until Amgarad found her."

Clara woke up at the sound of their voices and stared at her mother in disbelief. "Mum," she said, sitting up. "Oh, Mum!" And as she burst into tears, Mrs MacLean gathered her in her arms and held her tight. A set expression crossed her face. It was an expression her husband recognized immediately and Lord Rothlan, too, knew stubbornness when he saw it.

"I'm taking Clara back home with me right now, John," she said, "and I don't care what you say."

John MacLean looked at Lord Rothlan doubtfully.

"Actually, I think it's a very good idea, Janet," Lord Rothlan said, suddenly serious. "Clara came to no harm in the cave but the experience has shaken her a great deal. All she needs is rest and she'll be as right as rain, I promise you."

Clara got to her feet and wrapping her cloak around her, wiped the tears from her eyes. "I'm sorry," she muttered, feeling ashamed at her outburst. "It was just seeing Mum so unexpectedly ..."

Rothlan smiled understandingly. "You're just tired, Clara," he said, "and it's best that you go home with your mother." Suddenly thoughtful, he eyed the crow perched on the Ranger's shoulder. "I think you should take Kitor with you, too. It might be dangerous if the prince sees him with us."

Lady Ellan nodded. "That's a good idea," she said. "Keep him hidden under your cloak and take him into the hill when you get back, Clara. He'll be safe there."

Half an hour later, when goodbyes had been said and the carpet carrying Mrs MacLean, Clara and Kitor had floated out of earshot, the Ranger looked at Lord Rothlan. "Was it wise to let Clara go?" he questioned. "She knows the magic words, after all."

"We can rely on Neil for the magic words, John. They'll come into his mind when he needs them. Clara and Kitor are both better off in the hill. As long as the prince believes that Kitor is dead and Clara is still in the cave, it'll make him feel safe, and as long as he feels safe, he's not a threat — but if he'd seen Kitor with us and Clara still alive ..."

"You're right," the Ranger nodded, "I hadn't thought of it like that."

36. The Black Tower

"Well," said Lord Rothlan, reining in his horse at the top of a steep slope, "there it is! The Black Tower of Ardray and its magic forest!"

Neil gaped at it in wonder. Like Clara, he hadn't given much thought to what the Black Tower would look like and nothing that had been said had prepared him for the sight of the magnificent castle that dominated the landscape. Its smooth elegance left him speechless and he could only stare open-mouthed at the huge building whose towers and turrets swept majestically above the magic forest. The winged eagles perched on its balconies lent it a fairy-tale appeal that entranced him. Indeed the whole scene was totally mesmerizing for, despite the grim, snow-clad mountains that lay behind them, the hand of winter had not touched the forest. It too was beautiful; its trees swaying gently in a mild breeze, their undersides gleaming white and, dotted here and there, just as Kitor had described, were the round scarlet balls of creepers that hung among them like Christmas decorations.

"How are we for time, John?" Lord Rothlan asked, for the day was well advanced.

The Ranger looked at his watch. "It's quarter to three," he said. "If Sir James is right and the prince's meeting is at three then he ought to be setting off about now."

"Right, we can go ahead then. His meeting is important and he's not likely to miss it!"

Rothlan urged his horse forward and, as the other horses fell into line and picked their way delicately down the grassy slope, Neil looked at his father and saw that he, too, was looking in awed wonder at the Black Tower.

"If Kalman has a protective shield round the forest," Rothlan said, turning in the saddle when they reached level ground, "then we ought to encounter it about now. I think we should spread out and walk forward slowly."

Step by step, the horses moved in a line towards the first trees of the forest and then suddenly, tossing their heads in fright, took only a few steps more and stopped, sensing the barrier that lay ahead. Jaikie dismounted and, with hands outstretched, felt for the invisible wall that barred them from the forest.

"It's here, milord," he said.

"Right! Take the broomsticks off the horses," Rothlan instructed as he untied the rope that fastened his to the side of his saddle. "Can you manage yours, Ellan?"

Ellan laughed as she pulled her broomstick free of the horse's harness and sitting on it sideways, soared skywards.

The Ranger held his broomstick in his hand as he walked up to the invisible barrier and tried to touch it. He had thought that it would feel like glass but there was nothing there — it was completely invisible yet try as he might, he couldn't step through it. He turned to watch Neil who was circling on his broomstick. "Don't fool around, Neil," he admonished as Rothlan flew towards them. "Pay attention, for goodness sake!"

Rothlan hovered, feet from the ground, and looked round. Inside the magic barrier, the forest seemed to heave uneasily as though the trees sensed their danger.

"Now, Neil," Rothlan smiled reassuringly, "it's time for you to put your hands against the barrier and say the Sultan's magic words! Don't worry," he said, seeing Neil's suddenly anxious face, "they will be there and you will remember them!"

What happened next took them completely by surprise. Perhaps the quiet peacefulness of the scene lulled them into a sense of false security but, Neil thought afterwards, the real reason was that they had given no thought at all to what would happen when the barrier round the forest was removed. That said, Neil got off his broomstick as the others watched and, as soon as his hands touched the barrier, the magic words came smoothly and clearly into his mind, just as Rothlan had said they would.

"Kutaya Soloi!"

Even as he said them, the world around him erupted in an almighty shriek of sound that echoed horribly round the forest. The trees thrashed into life as the barrier suddenly disappeared and such was his surprise at the sudden violence confronting him that he lost his balance and stumbled forward.

His father grabbed him quickly as, with lightning speed, a red creeper shot from among the trees and wound itself round Neil's neck. Another and another followed, dragging the magic cloaks from their backs and winding themselves, like snapping elastic bands, round their arms and legs. Drawing his knife, the Ranger slashed at the creepers and, pulling Neil clear of the writhing tentacles, they ran towards their broomsticks. They had escaped, but at a price, for they left their cloaks in the forest and now had no protection against the puffs of white powder that were bursting from the trees.

Rothlan swooped towards them, covering his mouth and nose with his cloak as the air over the forest turned white in an explosion of sweet, poisonous spores.

"Hurry! Hurry!" he shouted urgently. "Get into the air! Quickly!"

At the first scream of sound, Hamish had immediately wheeled the horses round and taken them back up the hill at a gallop while Amgarad, a mere dot in the sky, watched keenly as, helped by Lord Rothlan, Neil and his father spiralled slowly upwards. Both were slumped dizzily over their broomsticks in the grip of a terrible sickness.

"Ellan! Jaikie! Look to the Ranger," Rothlan shouted as, flying alongside Neil, he put an arm round him to steady him. "Take deep breaths!" he said desperately. "Come on, as deep as you can," he urged, as Neil started to retch. "The air up here is fresh and clean. You must get rid of the poison before it affects your mind!"

The forest beneath them was now clouded in a mist of white powder through which they could see the snapping tendrils of creepers snaking upwards in the hope of catching them.

Rothlan, still clutching Neil in case he toppled off the broomstick, was grim-faced as he called the words of a spell. The hex hit the forest in a blast of wind and, as the trees bent against it, an eerie wail of sound shivered through the air. Looking down through a haze of nausea, Neil and the Ranger watched as the beautiful, evil trees started to wilt, shrivel and turn black. Amgarad, too, watched from on high and his sharp eyes saw, not only the death of the trees, but the myriad of strange, foul creatures that were revealed to the light.

Still clutching Neil, Lord Rothlan edged his broomstick round and guided them towards the smooth shining surface of the Black Tower. "Don't worry about the forest," he said grimly, "the trees will cause us no more harm. Come now — to the tower!"

As they flew closer to the looming bulk of the massive building Rothlan headed for the swirl of curved balconies guarded by the great, stone eagles. This, he knew, was their destination for, behind, the angled sweep of their outspread wings, lay the room of magic mirrors.

"Hold on tight and follow me in, Neil!" Rothlan instructed as he hexed a window open and flew inside, swinging round swiftly to help Neil as he landed. Jaikie and Ellan flew in on either side of the Ranger who, by now, was so ill that he could hardly stand. So concerned were they that they barely noticed the mirrors that curved round the stone walls of the turret-room. It was only when they lifted their heads to look around that realization dawned and they gasped in sheer amazement, unable to believe their eyes.

The crown was there! Reflected hundreds of times over in the circle of mirrors, it stood before them on an ornate stand of carved, black wood, radiating power and magnificence. A black, iron crown studded about with magnificent rubies that glowed a fiery red. The Sultan's Crown! They looked at one another in relief. At last they had found it!

37. Through the Looking Glass

Had the courier not been late that morning with the promised dispatches from Paris, Louis de Charillon would have arrived earlier at the grey, stone town house in Moray Place and the drama that was to follow might have turned out very differently indeed. On such small turns of fortune do great events sometimes hang.

As it was, the count hastily signed the courier's receipt and rang Ned Stuart to say that he was on his way with the documents. He looked at his watch briefly as he jumped into his car and headed for Moray Place. Almost a quarter to three. He hoped he wouldn't make Ned too late for his meeting.

"Louis, you brought them!" There was no mistaking Stuart's relief and gratitude as he took him into the study, slit open the package and ran his eyes over the papers. "These will make all the difference," he said, leafing through them delightedly. "I must admit, I was getting rather nervous about the time — I should have left a good five minutes ago. I hope they'll forgive me for being a bit late!"

"I won't keep you, Ned," de Charillon smiled, loosening his coat and perching on the arm of a chair. He laid his gloves on a side table as Stuart passed him one of the documents.

"This one ... this is the most important one," Stuart said, bending over him "you see, this proves the relationship ..."

The sudden shriek of sound that filled the room stopped him in mid-sentence. It was a dreadful, horrible noise. If the souls of the dead had cried from their graves the sound could not have been more fearful.

"What on earth was that noise?" gasped de Charillon, looking instinctively towards the window.

Stuart stood beside him, frozen to the ground, his face a stony mask.

"I ... I'm sorry, Louis," he said, jerking suddenly back to the present, "something's ... er, just cropped up ... I'm sorry, but really you'll have to leave," and, grasping him firmly by the elbow, Stuart almost frog-marched the startled count from the house.

Standing outside the front door and gazing around in a mixture of puzzlement and rising anger, for he was not used to such treatment, the count could see no reason for the dreadful noise. Indeed, Moray Place was reassuringly normal. Shivering in the cold, he fastened his coat and then realized to his annoyance that he had left his gloves inside the house.

Pursing his lips and cursing silently at being put in such a position, he hesitated to knock at the door after what had just happened and then noticed that in his haste to get him out of the house, Stuart had not shut it properly. Taking a deep breath, he pushed it open and seeing no one in the hall, ventured inside. They were, after all, an expensive pair of gloves and it would only take a few seconds to retrieve them. Feeling decidedly uncomfortable and a bit like a burglar, he tiptoed towards the study and, through its open door, was just in time to see Ned Stuart walk clean through one of the huge wall-mirrors that were fixed on either side of the window.

As he stepped into the room on the other side of the mirror, Prince Kalman stopped dead, his face a mask of disbelief as he saw the little group clustered round the crown. Rothlan froze at the sight of him and the others turned; absolutely thunder-struck at his sudden appearance!

Slim, elegant and handsome in a dark, beautifully-cut suit, his fair hair caught in a velvet bow at the nape of his neck and a square emerald glinting on his finger; he stood before them; the epitome of regal majesty.

It was obvious from his expression that he had not expected them to be in the tower. His amazement, however, showed only for an instant and quickly regaining his composure he favoured Lord Rothlan and Lady Ellan with a low bow before striding towards the crown.

"My dear Alasdair," he purred, his hands running in relief over the priceless rubies that were stuck all over the crown like plums in a pudding, "how very nice to see you again, after all this time."

Rothlan's eyes narrowed speculatively as he bowed in return. "The pleasure, Kalman, is all yours," he returned coldly.

The prince's face lost its affability, his expression changing swiftly to one of undisguised dislike. "As you know, Rothlan," he drawled insolently, "you've never been one of my favourite people." He paused, eying them all in turn. "And honesty compels me to point out that I didn't invite you here — neither you nor your friends! In fact," he said dryly, "it was just as well that you hexed the forest for it warned me of your arrival and at least gave me the opportunity of welcoming you to my humble abode."

Rothlan shrugged. "We didn't come here to enjoy your hospitality, Kalman, as you well know. We came to return the Sultan's Crown to its rightful owner."

The prince's chin lifted as his fingers tightened round the crown. "Ah, but it's mine now," he said with a smile, "and with its power, Scotland will soon become one of the greatest nations in the world and ..."

"And your friends the French?" interrupted Rothlan contemptuously. "Where do they come into the scheme of things?"

"Ah, the French!" Kalman gestured elegantly. "You are wrong to despise them, Rothlan," he said, mocking him gently. "They are, after all, a people of culture, elegance and grace."

"So are the Scots," countered Rothlan, "or have you forgotten that you are one of the Lords of the North? Why don't you give the crown back to the Turkish Sultan and bring back the old days of trust and friendship between us."

"Are you, by any chance, suggesting that I live a quiet life, Alasdair?" Kalman's lips sneered and his eyes hooded as he shook his head in mock amusement. "Don't be so naïve! I've spent years planning all this and I'm not going to give it up now!" He cradled the crown lovingly. "And for what?" he sneered. "My father and I decided long ago that the only thing worth having in this world is power and once I'm King of Scotland, I'll be able to do anything! Anything I please!" He smiled at the prospect. "And Scotland, I assure you, will only be the beginning! Such a pity, isn't it, that you and your friends will not be around to see my rise to power in the world — for I have great plans for the future, I assure you!"

When he saw Ned Stuart walk clean through the huge wall-mirror in his study, Louis de Charillon's eyes had very nearly popped out of his head. He stopped dead in his tracks, totally confused, as his brain told him what he had seen but his reason utterly rejected such an impossible occurrence.

Indeed, so intrigued was he that, after a quick glance round to check that no one was about, he walked up to the mirror and rather hesitantly touched the glass with his hands. It felt solid enough and, scanning the surrounds, he decided that it certainly didn't seem to be a door. As he stood looking at it in puzzled wonder, quite sure that he had not been mistaken in what he had just seen, he ran his hands over the ornate frame and felt one of the carved flowers slip gently under his fingers. He turned it curiously, thinking it was, perhaps, some sort of handle but as nothing happened he shrugged and, rather belatedly remembering that he was, after all, in someone else's house, he picked up his gloves and hastily left the study.

A shiver of cold air reminded him that he'd left the front door open and as he drew on his gloves, he saw Sir James Erskine in the hall with a pretty girl beside him. There was nothing remarkable about this except that his senses told him that not two seconds previously they had both been pigeons!

He broke into a cold sweat as he realized that his brain was not functioning quite as it should. People walking through mirrors and pigeons turning into people rang enough warning bells in his ordered mind to turn him white with shock. He felt his legs buckle under him and as he staggered suddenly, they rushed to catch him.

"Careful, Louis!" said Sir James, grasping his arm and steadying him. "Clara ... help me get him into the study."

"I ... I'm all right, James," de Charillon muttered weakly as they helped him to a chair. "It's just that ... I ... just for a moment, I thought you were ... pigeons!"

Clara smiled at him reassuringly. "There were some in the hall when we came in but maybe the sun was in your eyes," she said, blithely ignoring the fact that it was a dull, sunless, winter's day.

The count smiled thinly, not at all convinced, but rose and shook hands with them cordially enough as Sir James introduced Clara. "Have ... have you come to see Stuart?" he asked, turning to Sir James.

"After a fashion," nodded Sir James. "We were worried that he might be late for his meeting. He hasn't gone yet, has he? His car is still outside."

De Charillon took a deep breath. "You'll never believe this," he said, walking over to the mirror, "but the last I saw of him, he was walking through this mirror!"

Sir James and Clara both straightened in horror as he casually clicked one of the carvings round a couple of times. "I thought that the mirror might be some sort of door," he said, "and that this might be a handle, but it doesn't seem to do anything."

Sir James spoke through lips that had gone suddenly stiff. "No, it doesn't, does it."

"I don't think it can be a door anyway," Clara said consideringly, her eyes still round with shock, "it's ... it's on an outside wall."

"You're right, of course," smiled the count somewhat shakily. "I think I must have imagined it all. Really, if you don't mind, I'm feeling a bit confused. I ... I ought to be getting along now."

Two perfectly ordinary pigeons were fluttering aimlessly round the hall as they made their way towards the door.

"Oh, look! They can't get out, poor things," Clara said, flapping her hands at them. De Charillon, nevertheless, threw them a glance of deep suspicion as she opened the door wide and shooed them into the street.

The count bowed formally as he said goodbye but his mind was racing. He was not a fool and knew perfectly well that something quite out of the ordinary was going on, but for the life of him he couldn't quite work out what — and as magic didn't for a second enter into his calculations, he put his car into gear and headed for home, none the wiser.

38. Winner Takes All

From the moment the prince had stepped through the mirror into the tower, Rothlan had kept the prince talking in the hope that Neil would remember the magic words that would free the crown from Kalman's power. Neil, however, remained silent and as the prince eyed them all speculatively, Rothlan was forced to turn and look at the white-faced boy who stood, pale and staring vacantly, by his side.

Prince Kalman followed his glance and gave an ugly laugh as his astute brain told him what had happened.

"So the Sultan didn't trust you, Alasdair!" he gloated. "He trusted a couple of children instead! How very galling for you, my dear! And the boy has the sickness of the forest on him."

Rothlan's heart sank. He glanced hopelessly at Ellan who, still clutching her broomstick, had turned her head to look at the top of the staircase. Jaikie, too, seemed distracted by a light, rustling noise but at the prince's words, both looked at Neil and the Ranger and shook their heads slightly. It was obvious that they were totally oblivious to what was going on around them. They had lost their memories and the sickness of the trees was raging within them.

The Prince lifted the crown from its stand and, holding it triumphantly in the curve of his arm, seemed to grow in stature. "You chose a rather inopportune moment to try to steal my crown," he said casually, "but as you doubtless know, I have quite an important meeting to attend this afternoon. I'm late already and as I've no intention of missing it you will forgive me if I hex you out of this world, won't you?"

Rothlan vaguely heard the rustling noise become louder but, totally absorbed by Kalman's words, he ignored it. His lips tightened to a thin line in the knowledge that his magic was powerless against that of the crown and as bleak despair shaded his eyes, Kalman lifted his arm to hex them. Meeting the courage in Rothlan's eyes, however, he hesitated, realizing with a stab of anguish that over the years he had allowed his jealousy of Rothlan to cloud his judgement. They had been friends as boys. It shouldn't end like this, he thought suddenly and as their eyes held, he hesitated to speak the words of the hex.

It was his undoing, for it was then that the goblins arrived. Forced into the light from their deep dens in the roots of the forest, they had headed in a maddened rush for the darkness of the tower. Half-blind and driven almost insane by the sunlight, they rose in a rustling, rippling tide up its narrow, spiral staircase and streamed into the topmost room in a flood of dry, disgusting, stinking bodies. Kalman, totally unprepared for such an invasion, turned in surprise as, totally disorientated, they rushed in, roaring and slobbering horribly, their razor-sharp fingernails like daggers.

"Hit the ceiling," shouted Rothlan as he kicked out at the goblins that were tearing at his cloak. No one needed a second telling, even Neil and the Ranger, sick as they were, flew up out of the goblins' reach. Two of them, however, managed to grasp Jaikie's broomstick as he lifted off the ground and despite his efforts to shake them off, they clung on determinedly. Kicking out at them in a frantic attempt to break their grasp, Jaikie was so busy trying to fend them off that he totally forgot to look where he was going and, in the excitement of the moment, accidentally flew clean through one of the mirrors — goblins and all!

Emerging in Kalman's study in Moray Place, Jaikie swerved instinctively to avoid hitting someone standing in his way and, to his amazement, found that it was Sir James that he'd almost knocked to the ground.

As the surprised goblins released their hold and he swept round the unfamiliar room, he realized what must have happened and saw, to his joy, that it not only contained Sir James, but Clara as well!

Relief flooded through him. Help was at hand.

Clara gulped as Jaikie and two huge, ugly green creatures that stank to the heavens, blasted their way through the mirror, causing Sir James to duck hastily. She didn't know that they were goblins; it was enough that they were horrible, monstrous things with red eyes and long teeth that curved from slavering mouths. Their skin, gnarled and knobbly like the bark of very old trees, hung off them in folds and rustled dryly as they hopped around trying to catch Jaikie, who by this time was hovering near the ceiling, dodging round the crystals of an ornate chandelier in an effort to escape their claw-like fingers.

Scrambling to his feet, Sir James shoved Clara towards the door before grabbing a shovel from the fireplace and entering the fray.

"Be careful you don't go through the other mirror," Clara yelled at Jaikie as he whizzed round the room with the goblins dancing with rage below him, "the setting's been altered!"

"Chase the goblins through it if you can then," Jaikie said, circling the room.

Sir James solved the problem by stepping forward, hitting both the surprised goblins over the head with the shovel and chucking them both through the mirror. Before they could come back, Jaikie flew down and, with a sigh of relief, twisted the rose-shaped carving.

"Thank goodness!" he said, as he locked the mirror firmly. "Now they can't get back in!"

Sir James, tie askew and panting with exertion, dropped the shovel. "What the devil is going on, Jaikie?" he demanded.

"It's a disaster!" whispered Jaikie, running his hand through his hair. "A complete and utter disaster! Neil's lost his memory, Kalman has the crown and we're being attacked by those goblins from the magic forest!"

"Neil's lost his memory?" Clara gasped.

"Yes," Jaikie nodded. "Clara, I know it's dangerous but only you know the magic words. You've got to come with me through the mirror!"

"We'll both come," Sir James said grimly, taking Clara's hand. "You go first, Jaikie, and we'll follow."

Magnified endlessly by the circle of mirrors, the scene that met their eyes seemed one of total carnage. While Rothlan, Lady Ellan and the others hovered high above them, Kalman was hexing the goblins frantically but even though their bodies littered the room, a seemingly unending tide of newcomers welled up from the staircase, clambering unheedingly over the bodies of their comrades, to join in the fight.

Rothlan gasped with relief as he saw Clara and Sir James step through one of the mirrors and realizing that the situation had changed for the better, promptly threw a few hexes of his own to quell the goblins.

Prince Kalman looked at him in surprise and then swung round as he saw the newcomers.

Clara's arrival stopped him in his tracks. He froze as she stepped towards him and although she met his cold, blue eyes bravely, she quailed at the power that

radiated from him. He was every inch a king despite
his scratched face and torn clothes; and he still held
the crown.

"Ah!" he said, an odd expression on his face, "so you
survived, did you? That was my mistake! I should have
finished you off with Kitor!"

Clara flinched at his words and, before he could hex
her, spoke the Sultan's magic words: *"Kutaya Soloi."*

They came clearly and easily to her lips and such
were the ringing tones of the spell that even the goblins
stopped in their tracks and looked at her in amazement.

Her words were accompanied by a sudden, tremendous bang and a flash of light that stunned them all.
Understanding dawned as, before their astonished
eyes, the Turkish Sultan materialized in all his finery
with his entourage behind him.

The goblins took one look at the sharp, curved scimitars of the Sultan's guards and decided wisely that, at
this stage of the proceedings, discretion was undoubtedly the better part of valour. They exchanged speaking
glances and then, very quietly, eased themselves out of
the room, fled down the staircase and were never seen
or heard of again.

Such was the charged atmosphere in the room of
mirrors, however, that no one noticed them go. The
prince stood rigid, paralysed with fear, as the Sultan
approached him and, with a stern face, took the crown
from his nerveless fingers. "My crown, I think!" he said
in a voice of iron.

The prince's lips closed in a thin, hard line and his
eyes were bleak as his dreams of power and grandeur
collapsed around him. Rothlan and Lady Ellan looked
at one another apprehensively, knowing that the
Sultan's punishment would be both fitting and fairly

dreadful. Kalman knew it, too, and as the power of the crown drained from him and reverted to the Sultan, he was left increasingly bereft and defenceless. He did not lack courage, however, and even as his features weakened and his personality diminished, he tried desperately to hide his fear and keep the remains of his dignity.

It was Amgarad, however, who forced him into his final, fatal move; for, hearing the noise of battle emanating from the tower, he had flown down to defend his master. Swooping like an avenging angel through the window, Amgarad, instead, came face to face with the prince; the prince who, until recently, had condemned him to live for years in the filthy body of a monstrous bird.

Recognition was instant and such was his hatred of Kalman that he launched himself on him with a scream of fury. The prince staggered back under the onslaught, trying to protect his eyes from Amgarad's raking talons. It was the knowledge that he couldn't shake him off, as well as the realization that not one of those present would do anything to help him, that made him turn towards the mirrors.

"Damn you! Damn you all!" he screamed, and, turning suddenly, he threw himself into the mirror behind him.

Jaikie, always quick off the mark, rushed forward and, with a quick twist, turned the carving that locked the mirror. Sweat dripped from him as he laid his face against the glass and slid down to his knees, shaking at what he had achieved and hardly able to believe that he had been in time.

Sir James finally broke the silence. "I ... I don't think Prince Kalman will trouble us any more," he said quietly. "Jaikie's just trapped him between mirrors!"

"Has he, by God," Rothlan said, his eyes sharp. "Then we must leave here at once before Ardray disintegrates! Quickly, everyone, through the other mirror! Ellan," he turned to her, "quickly, gather up all the broomsticks, we can't leave them here!"

As Rothlan urged Clara and Sir James back through the mirror, the Sultan walked over to Jaikie who was bent over the Ranger and Neil.

"Neil and the Ranger have both lost their memories, your majesty," he said worriedly. "They lost their cloaks in the magic forest."

The Sultan rested the crown on the Ranger's head, then on Neil's and spoke the words of a spell. Even as they watched, his magic words wrought a miracle. Colour flowed back into their white faces and their eyes brightened as the sickness of the trees left them. They barely had time to look around when the tower shivered and seemed to slip slightly. It was enough! Jaikie hastily grabbed them and hurried them through the mirror.

The Sultan, holding the crown before him like a talisman, turned to Lord Rothlan. "We have little time for discussion," he said quickly, "for this accursed place will soon be gone. I will make my own way home from here and will be in touch with you later through the crystal."

Rothlan nodded. "Your horses are safe, your majesty. They served us well and you have our thanks."

"And you have my thanks, Alasdair," he said, "my very grateful thanks. Rest assured that I and the power of my crown will always be at your service."

Another slight tremor shook the Black Tower of Ardray and knowing that the prince's entire estate was about to disappear, Lord Rothlan bowed swiftly to the Sultan and, with Amgarad on his shoulder, stepped through the magic mirror into Ned Stuart's study in Moray Place.

The Sultan, holding fast to the crown, muttered a few magic words and, seconds later, he and his entourage materialized beside a startled Hamish who, hearing the initial rumble of sound from Ardray and knowing what it portended, had jumped to his feet in alarm.

"They are all quite safe," the Sultan told him quickly, seeing the fear in his eyes, "and, as you see, the crown has been returned to me."

Hamish bowed low.

"And the prince, your majesty? Prince Kalman?"

"He is caught between mirrors and will not trouble us again."

Hamish gave a sigh of relief.

The Sultan smiled. "I am taking my horses back to their stables at Ruksh," he said. "The storm carriers will carry them there on the wings of the wind. And one of them will carry you back to your hill in Edinburgh. You will convey my regards to the MacArthur and inform him that I will be in touch with him soon. I have much to be grateful for!"

Hamish bowed again and watched as the storm carriers darkened the sky in hues of brown and purple and in a swirl of wind, gathered the horses in their great arms and bore them off.

39. Fish out of Water

The violent storm that raged across Scotland that afternoon took even the weathermen by surprise. Indeed, it seemed to blow up out of nothing, came from nowhere, defied every rule of meteorology and hammered the entire country. It swept in from the northwest, raced across the Highlands, buffeted Glasgow, howled through Edinburgh and, much to the Prime Minister's delight, sent the French fishing fleet in the North Sea, racing for home.

Edinburgh was, perhaps, the hardest hit. Thunder rumbled ominously from a sky that had become as black as ink and the breathless wind that soughed over its cobbled streets stirred gradually from a strange unease to a tearing blast. Spears of rain lashed the city and lightning jagged in vicious streaks through the evil-looking clouds that tumbled and rolled over the castle in shades of brown, purple and black. The wind shrieked and howled through the streets for hours on end, rattling windows and ripping to shreds the tartan banners that decorated the city, leaving it clean and clear of Prince Kalman's spell.

It was well into the middle of the night, when the storm had passed over and swept into the North Sea, that the wind eased and, into the sudden, breathless stillness, fell the first flakes of snow. The huge, soft, heavy flakes that drifted gently over town and country, coated the land in a thick blanket of white and the people of Scotland woke next morning to a silent, snow-covered landscape that gleamed under a clear, blue, winter sky.

"Well, MacArthur," Sir James smiled, stretching out on a long sofa in the Great Hall under Arthur's Seat, "thank goodness that's all over and done with!"

The MacArthur, carefully avoiding Lady Ellan's frowning glance, lit his pipe, settled himself comfortably among the cushions on his high chair and blew clouds of smoke into the air. "Aye," he said contentedly, "we've achieved a lot and maybe now we'll have some peace. Prince Kalman has gone for good and Scotland is safe from his magic." He paused, eyeing them all smilingly. "The Sultan, too, is relieved at the way things have ended. He spoke to me this morning through the crystal and sends you his thanks and an invitation to spend the New Year in Turkey — an invitation that I accepted on your behalf."

There was an excited murmur at this. "A holiday," said Sir James, "is just what we all need! Nobody can say we don't deserve it!"

"Sun, sand and blue sky," murmured Clara, "fabulous!"

"And the food," added Neil. "I loved it — the kebabs, the salads, the stuffed vine-leaves, the ..."

"What, no haggis?" teased his mother.

"Mum, don't ever feed me haggis again! Honestly, I've had enough to last me a lifetime!"

"That's certainly one thing that we can be grateful for," grinned Clara. "No more haggis and tartan!"

Her father smiled in agreement. "It's really quite funny when you think back on it all! The whole of Scotland was positively plastered in tartan for months and everyone thought it wonderful! Goodness knows what the tourists thought!"

"Or the English," added the Chief Constable with a sly smile at George Tatler.

Tatler laughed. "It was absolutely mind-boggling," he admitted, "and I can't tell you how relieved I am that that storm blew down all those dreadful tartan banners."

"Oh, that was deliberate," Hamish grinned. "The storm carrier that brought me back from Ardray was an obliging chap so we asked him for a favour! It didn't take him long to get rid of them!"

The Chief Constable's eyes narrowed. "You mean you called up that storm? You can control the weather?"

At this, Arthur blew smoke down his nose and Archie grinned and nodded lazily from his favourite position in the crook of the dragon's arm. "Well, some of the time," he nodded. "When it's necessary!"

"Like the handy mist that Arthur brewed up, eh?" Tatler smiled at the great dragon. He leant forward. "You know, the French are still in total shock over what happened to their fleet. It'll take them months to get over it! Officially, there's no comment but rumours are spreading! Rumours are spreading!" he repeated with some glee.

"And what about the French fishermen?" enquired the Ranger, who sat beside Sir James with Kitor perched on his shoulder. "What happened to them? I read in the papers that the storm forced them back to port and most of the boats lost all their gear and were badly damaged!"

The MacArthur choked into his pipe and had a fit of coughing. "Aye," he said, wiping his eyes, "they got back to port by the skin of their teeth, I've no doubt, but I made sure they had a really tough time of it before they got there! Just to teach them a wee lesson not to meddle with the Scots in future, ye ken! I asked yon storm carrier to frighten the wits out of them, all the way back to France and, by God, he did a grand job. A grand job! They'll not be coming back here again for many a long day, believe me!"

The Ranger looked doubtful. "I wouldn't bank on it, MacArthur. Fishing is big business, you know, and everyone's in it for the money."

The MacArthur smiled and waved his pipe. "They won't come back," he assured him. "You see," he confessed, "I ... er, I added another spell to Arthur's little bag of tricks when he went out to hex the French fleet."

"What was that?" queried Sir James, looking a trifle apprehensive.

"Well," he gloated, "I hexed their nets, didn't I?"

"Hexed their nets!" Amgarad fluttered to keep his balance as Rothlan straightened in his chair and looked at Sir James in alarm.

The MacArthur sat back and looked at them all mischievously. "Ocht, it was nothing to worry about. Just a wee bit of fun!"

"A wee bit of fun!" Ellan looked at Rothlan helplessly.

"Aye, it was the funniest thing you ever saw," he assured them. "You see, I got a bit bored with you all away on your adventures and the like so I hexed their nets and watched what happened through the crystal."

"And what *did* happen, MacArthur?" asked Tatler, sitting forward on the edge of his chair.

The MacArthur's lips twitched. "Well, at first they couldn't believe it — but when it happened time after time, well ..."

"When *what* happened time after time, father?"

"Man, were they furious!" reminisced the MacArthur, chuckling at the thought. "You should have heard the language!" He shook his head. "Dreadful, dreadful!"

"Father!" Lady Ellan said warningly.

He leant forward. "I'll tell you what happened. They were out there for days, you know — days and days — and in all that time, they didn't catch one single fish! Not one *fish,* not one *crab,* not one *any-thing! That's* what happened! Every time they pulled their nets in, they came up empty; completely and utterly empty!"

"You mean ... they caught no fish? No fish at all?" stuttered Sir James.

"Not one!" The MacArthur sat back proudly. "Believe me, they were swearing all the way back to France."

Tatler gave a whinny of sheer glee that set them all off and even Arthur's great body heaved with laughter at the completeness of their victory against the French.

Tatler wiped his eyes. "I wondered why the fisher-men had it in for Marcel Bruiton," he gasped, "and now I know! The North Sea fiasco was all his idea and by heavens, they were out for his blood. After all the demonstrations in Paris he's had to resign, you know. It's not official yet. They'll be announcing it tomorrow, I think."

"Good riddance to him," opined Sir James.

"Ocht, I wouldn't blame Bruiton too much," the MacArthur said slowly. "Kalman used the crown's magic to control him, after all. *He* made him send the French fishermen out in the first place and sending the navy in after them was just a ploy to distract atten-tion from his bid for the throne of Scotland. And don't forget, he needed French co-operation to have all those ancestral documents of his authenticated as well."

Tatler nodded in agreement. "You're right," he con-firmed. "I found out just the other day that it was one of Bruiton's chaps that verified them."

"But Kalman wasn't really Bonnie Prince Charlie's son, was he?" frowned Neil.

"Of course not," Lord Rothlan said smiling, "he trav-elled back in time just as we did and forged the birth certificate and all the other documents that he would need to prove his claim.

The MacArthur nodded. "I think it was the knowledge that you were on your way to get the crown, Alasdair, that forced his hand. His big mistake was to try and hurry things along but if he'd only waited and gone through the proper channels, the documents would have been authenticated eventually, for scientific analysis would have shown that the paper and ink were all of the correct period."

"Anyway," said Tatler, "the new chap that's replacing Bruiton seems very capable and much more reasonable. I hear he went to school with Louis de Charillon."

"In that case, I wouldn't mind betting that the count will probably end up an ambassador!" muttered the Chief Constable. "Sooner rather than later!"

"Probably," agreed Sir James. "And he'll make a good job of it, too. But, you know, we're seriously going to have to do something about him. He not only saw Ned Stuart going through that magic mirror but he also saw Clara and me demerging from a couple of pigeons."

"What about a memory spell?" queried Lord Rothlan.

Sir James looked at Tatler and the Chief Constable. "I think a memory spell would be an insult to someone of that calibre," he said slowly. "He suspects a lot and although he's been questioned about it, he hasn't mentioned seeing me at Moray Place that afternoon, has he Archie?"

The Chief Constable shook his head. "Not a word. As far as he's concerned he gave Stuart the papers and left the house more or less immediately because he knew Stuart was in a hurry to get to the meeting and was late already. Totally feasible with no one around to prove or disprove his story."

"What puzzles me is that no one is making a fuss about Ned Stuart's disappearance," said Neil. "I mean, everyone was *for* him! There was going to be a grand parade down the High Street. They even said that he was going to live in Holyrood Palace after he was crowned ... but now ..."

"Yes," agreed Clara, "we've been looking in the newspapers and there's no mention of him. You'd think the papers would be full of it!"

"Was *that* a memory spell, sir?" Neil said, bouncing up straight on his cushion.

"Not in the way you mean," smiled Lord Rothlan. "You see, when the Sultan took the crown from him, Kalman lost his power and the Scottish spell, remember, was his. Now that it has faded away, Stuart will become just a vague memory and I doubt if any one will remember much of the ins and outs of the affair."

"What about the house in Moray Place and the magic mirrors?" queried Mrs MacLean.

"The house didn't belong to Kalman," Sir James answered. "I made some enquiries about that. He rented it from an Edinburgh lawyer who has a holiday house somewhere in Spain. I went to visit him and found him a bit absent-minded, but apart from being totally confused as to why he'd spent a couple of years in Spain instead of six months, there seems to be no harm done."

"And the magic mirrors?" queried Neil.

"Ah! The mirrors! Yes, I asked him about the mirrors. Said I'd noticed them when I'd been invited to the house and would like to buy them. He'd tried to return them, apparently, but as he couldn't get in touch with Ned Stuart he'd ended up sending them to the sale rooms to be auctioned. I checked up on that, of course, but the company that bought them seems to have gone out of business."

"So they've disappeared?"

Sir James nodded and glanced at the MacArthur. "Maybe they were meant to fade out of the picture, I don't know, but I have a suspicion that it'll be the same with all the odd things that have happened, like the craze for tartan and the bagpipes. Although people will think it strange that they bought so much haggis, they'll just think that they had a taste for it and eaten so much of it that they can't face any more."

"You're right," agreed Mrs MacLean, "the shops are selling off their haggis, shortbread and Dundee cake at very reasonable prices and, do you know, I just can't bring myself to buy any."

"I'll guarantee that by the New Year, Ned Stuart and the tartan craze will have been completely forgotten," agreed the Chief Constable. "People have scrapped it already. All they're interested in now is Christmas shopping and what to wear at the office party. I see from the headlines in today's *Scotsman* that the Council has gone into gear for the winter celebrations. They've already started laying the ice rink in the gardens below the castle."

"Clara and I always go skating," Neil said, his face lighting up at the thought of the days ahead. "It's magic! They sell roast chestnuts and stuff."

Rothlan looked over at them and smiled at their enthusiasm. They had already shrugged off the dangers they had gone through and it was a relief to him that everything had turned out for the best. He watched as Amgarad stalked in his ungainly way over to Clara and his great wings flapped as he scrambled onto her shoulder. He would miss her when they returned to Jarishan. But Clara would have Kitor to keep her company and his eyes moved to where the crow perched perkily on the Ranger's shoulder.

The crow's bright glance met his in sparkling gratitude for he knew that it had been at Rothlan's suggestion that he should live with the Ranger and his family in Edinburgh. Everyone knew that Jarishan was the home of Amgarad and the eagles and, like Rothlan, Kitor knew that he would never have fitted in there.

And now he had a home in the park! Although he'd tried hard to tell them, neither Clara nor Neil would ever know the depth of the joy he'd felt when the Ranger had asked him if he'd like to stay with them. It was a dream! A family to live with and a home of his own; and not any ordinary home, but a home in the park — with cars passing backwards and forwards all day long and fast food on the doorstep! Never in his wildest dreams had he thought that such good fortune could be his. Kitor ruffled his feathers and sighed happily. Life could hold no more.

40. Tales of Fantasy

"Ah, yes," the young assistant behind the counter said deferentially, "your tiepin, Monsieur le Comte! It's all ready for you!" He picked a velvet box from a drawer and opened it for the count to see.

Louis de Charillon took the box in his hand and ran his fingers over the tiepin. Small and delicate, it had been beautifully made and although slightly different from the design he had submitted there was, nevertheless, a grace and elegance of line that spoke of the skill of a master craftsman.

"Mr Grant treated the feathers, Monsieur le Comte, with a special substance that will keep them from spoiling. Grouse feathers, aren't they? It's certainly a most unusual piece. Very striking!"

De Charillon clipped the tiepin onto his tie and, as he wrote the cheque, felt a sudden sense of well-being. He was glad he'd kept the feathers that his little grouse had left behind and had the strangest feeling that his new tiepin was going to bring him luck.

Feeling more relaxed that he had done in weeks, he paused to fasten his overcoat as he left the jewellers, for although the thin rays of winter sunshine bathed George Street in light, they did little to raise the near freezing temperature of an Edinburgh winter.

"My dear Louis, how nice to see you!"

"Sir James!" De Charillon's face cleared. "How are you?"

Hands were shaken all round as Sir James introduced Thompson and Tatler. "I think you know Archie Thompson, our Chief Constable? And George Tatler?"

The Count bowed. "Your servant, sir," he said, assessing him shrewdly.

"Christmas shopping?" queried Sir James with a smile, indicating the expensive trinkets that decorated the plate-glass windows of Hamilton & Inches, Edinburgh's most prestigious jeweller.

"You could say that," de Charillon allowed. He indicated the tiepin. "A present to myself!"

Sir James raised his eyebrows. "Very unusual," he said, looking at it closely. "Grouse feathers, aren't they?"

"Yes," de Charillon looked at them all speculatively and despite himself felt a strange sense of affinity creep over him, "they're all that was left of my little grouse before he ... er, became an eagle." And he knew, even as the words left his mouth, that what he had said was no surprise to them.

A flicker of understanding seemed to pass between the three men and Sir James nodded. "You know, I rather think we owe you a good lunch, Louis. If you have no other engagement we would be delighted to have you join us."

De Charillon was not a fool. Although their faces showed no more than casual politeness there was a shade of guardedness there too and he sensed that this was more than an invitation to lunch. He fingered his tiepin and again felt that same sense of comradeship. It was more like being asked to join a club.

He looked at them and they looked back, waiting for his reply.

"Gentlemen," he said, taking a deep breath, "I would be delighted."

"Wonderful," said Sir James, "the car is just over there. Tatler's invited us to The Witchery so we're heading for the High Street."

"Nice place," smiled the Chief Constable, "interesting name, too!"

"I've heard of it," de Charillon nodded. "It's full of old things about witchcraft and ... and magic."

Perhaps it was the grouse feathers that served to sharpen de Charillon's perception but he stopped abruptly and met Sir James's eyes in sudden understanding as quite a few things that had been puzzling him, clicked suddenly into place.

Sir James raised his eyebrows and, casting a quick glance at the other two men, smiled at the count somewhat ruefully.

"Lunch first, Louis," he grinned.

"And explanations afterwards, eh!" added the Chief Constable.

It was Tatler, however, who had the last word.

"After all," he nodded, his eyes twinkling at the totally stunned expression on de Charillon's face, "when you think about it, there's probably no better place in Edinburgh than The Witchery for telling faery stories."